A PAST PROBLEM

A PAST PROBLEM

GRAYSON SCOTT

TATE PUBLISHING
AND ENTERPRISES, LLC

A Past Problem

Published by Tate Publishing & Enterprises, LLC
127 E. Trade Center Terrace | Mustang, Oklahoma 73064 USA
1.888.361.9473 | www.tatepublishing.com

Tate Publishing is committed to excellence in the publishing industry. The company reflects the philosophy established by the founders, based on Psalm 68:11,
"The Lord gave the word and great was the company of those who published it."

Cover design by Rodrigo Adolfo
Interior design by Caypeeline Casas

Published in the United States of America

ISBN: 978-1-62510-377-2
1. category:sub category
2. category: sub category
13.07.26

To Mrs. Pam Bandy for teaching me not to tell myself the sky's the limit when there are footprints on the moon. For believing in me when others might have thought me crazy, and reading (more than a few times) every rendition that I came up with. Here's to the person who inspired my dreams. While others might only see you as an English teacher, I see you for what you really are: truly and fully great.

ACKNOWLEDGMENTS

To all my family, friends, and teachers who offered support and encouragement during the process of writing *A Past Problem*, I am extremely appreciative.

I am especially thankful for:

Pam Bandy—Thank you for being more than a teacher to not just me, but all of your students. What you started in eighth grade with a simple assignment has become my passion and dream. I couldn't have gotten here without you and everything that you have done for me and with me. You are more than a teacher, you are a friend. (P.S. I'm pretty sure you are to blame for getting me hooked on Sherlock Holmes.)

Dad and Mom—Your support through this has been invaluable. I'm pretty sure that I would still be rewriting chapter one if not for all of the encouragement that you two have provided.

Mitchell, Parker, and Aubrey—I couldn't ask for better siblings! Thanks for all of the encouragement and for not thinking that I was crazy for trying to write a book in the first place.

CONTENTS

THE METHODOLOGY OF DETECTIVE SMITH

The public may well be familiar with the name of Detective Smith and the many cases that he participated in. Only a spare few made it to print, usually appearing as a few paragraph articles in a popular newspaper. I myself had read these accounts and realized, with no small amount of admiration, the skill with which this man approached the investigative trade. Even more shocking is the fact that Detective Smith is not a true detective employed by any one police department, but is rather a freelancer, working only when approached by those in need of his skill set. This needs to be kept in mind. If any aspect of this story rings untrue, then you shall have to take it up with the very man himself, for everything here comes directly from his mouth to my ears. Before I go about explaining my relationship with this extraordinary man, I must write one or two key points to the public. In my travels, I stumbled across many of the notes that Detective Smith wrote in regard to his cases. The eyes of many of the readers of this excerpt will recognize with little effort the familiarities of the passages. Two of the stories made headlines, but ironically, the beginning of the chain of events that I am about to reveal did not. It does not possess me to unmask my identity at this time. I take up my pen for one reason only: to sort out, in their due order, the events revolving around the escape of a very dangerous man. It is with this goal in mind that I launch into a series of stories that will no doubt captivate my readers and lend a telling eye into the life of one Detective Smith.

The town where Detective Smith resided had had a stroke of good luck. The crime rate had declined significantly in the past few months and was expected to continue into the following as well. The peacefulness was a complete contrast to the beginning of the summer. Cases had flown into Smith's hands with such rapidity that he had to delegate many of them to his trusted assistant, Riley Stevens. Smith had been acquainted with Riley for some time and could rely upon his well-honed perceptivity. Because of this trust, it was not difficult for Detective Smith to send his right-hand man into a neighboring town to lend a hand on a case. It was common when crime was down to help with cases in nearby towns. The chief inspector, Henry Bollard, had also traveled with Riley to assist the local sheriff. Smith had felt glad that he finally had a period of rest—that is, until he got the call to fly down and give consulting advice to the two crime solvers. In no time at all, Detective Smith was waiting with luggage in hand at the Durango Airport. While he waited for his two companions, Smith surveyed his surroundings. Boxed in on all sides by mountains, the valley town was a perfect place for a vacation. He docketed this in his memory banks as a good vacation spot. His business, however, resided in an even smaller town named Pagosa Springs. Established in 1891 due to its close proximity to a host of natural sulfur springs, the town attracted quite the revenue from nation wide tourism. It, like its neighbor, is also located in a valley, with the San Juan Mountains hemming in the town from all angles. Its official location belongs in Archuleta County, one of the many counties that pepper the landscape of the state of Colorado. As he was thinking, a small car pulled up to the curb.

"Detective Smith! It's been too long!" a loud voice bellowed out of the driver side door. The door in question sprung open, and the chief inspector hopped out. He shoved out his hand, and the detective shook it. Henry Bollard had a heftier frame when compared to Smith's thin, sleek physique. He was not quite large, but not quite fit either. His face had a hardened aspect to it, almost as if it once was jovial but was reduced to something less when confronted with the harshness of crime.

"Why, hello, Chief! I am glad that an opportunity has arisen in which we get to work together once more," Smith said with a smile. The other door slammed shut, and Riley Stevens peered around the car.

"This one's quite the thinker, boss," he remarked.

"Ah yes, the case. From what I gather, this is quite the situation that we have before us."

"Spot on, Detective. I guess I'd better start at the beginning. About a month ago, a hundred-thousand-dollar diamond-encrusted purse from La Porte-

Monnaie was stolen from a home belonging to one Mrs. Jenkins. No alarm was given, no lock forced. Not a sound was heard from any of the neighbors, eliminating any possible witness. In a nutshell, we have a lot of hardworking people getting nowhere fast," the chief concluded, a hint of frustration in his tone.

"Impressive. Was anything gained from looking inside the locks?"

"Nope, except that whoever broke in had to have known the code," Riley jumped in.

"Then we are left with two possibilities. Either the culprit was exceptional with electronics, or he or she was close enough to Mrs. Jenkins to attain the code, if there was one," Detective Smith explained. No other points were given until the car pulled up to a sign labeled "Welcome to Pagosa Springs! Pop. 1,591 as of the 2000 census." Smith figured that the population was a little outdated, considering the recent boom in tourism that had occurred over the past twelve years.

"I don't know why this is so difficult. Only sixteen hundred people in the whole town and we have run the trail cold," the chief remarked with a shake of the head.

"I hope we catch this guy soon. It just doesn't feel right knowing that there is a criminal in such a tiny, peaceful town," Riley added. The gang drove through the town for about ten minutes before finally coming to a house that was nestled into the mountainside.

"Mrs. Jenkins house, I presume?" Smith asked. The chief nodded and pointed to the house that was just visible over the mountain.

"Mrs. Jenkins was at a friend's house during the break-in."

"Her house was being fumigated," Riley said, answering the unasked question.

"And the workmen did not perceive anything odd?" Smith asked.

"Strangely enough, they said that they were going to wait until the following week to do it. Funky timing, if you ask me," the chief explained.

"I would have to concur."

The chief inspector jumped out of the car and walked up the driveway of Mrs. Jenkins's house with Riley and Smith close on his heels. As the chief swung open the front door, Smith noticed that his estimate on a code being required for the alarm system was spot on. "Chief? Did the sheriff say anything about a signal being received on the night of the crime?"

The chief thought for a bit, sifting through the information in his head. "No, Detective. Nothing was reported until that morning when Mrs. Jenkins dialed the police. Why do you ask?"

"I happen to be a connoisseur of alarm systems, and this particular edition sends a signal to the nearest police station if any damage is recorded on the surface. Since no such signal was raised, it opens up an interesting inquiry."

"I take that it's time to speak to Mrs. Jenkins, Detective?" Riley asked.

"Indeed, my friend."

On their way out of the house, the chief dialed up Mrs. Jenkins and asked her to meet the three of them at the nearby coffee shop. As the car pulled in to the River Point Café, a tall woman with a large, purple-feathered hat was waiting for them by the door.

"Detective Smith, I was wondering when I would meet you," Mrs. Jenkins said.

"I apologize, but you have me at a disadvantage."

"Your assistant has spoken very highly of you, Detective."

"I see. The fact that Riley has been down here awhile escaped me," Smith said with a nod.

"What do you need from me?" Mrs. Jenkins asked. The three of them looked at one another and silently agreed that Riley should be the one to initiate the questioning.

"We just wanted to ask you a few questions about the people that you know."

"What about them?" she responded with a touch of harshness. It was evident that this train of questions had been asked numerous times.

"We have suitable reasons to believe that one of them may have stolen your purse," the chief said.

"I can't see why."

The chief began to answer but was interrupted by his cell phone. A few hurried words were spoken before he turned back toward the group. "I'm sorry Detective, but something just came up. Some lunatic decided that it would be funny to smash into a jewelry store with his massive two-cylinder truck and rob the place. The clerk was so surprised that he fainted, and the guy got away. Well, they're shorthanded and need me."

"No problem, Chief. I wish you the best of luck," Smith said, shaking hands with the chief inspector. He watched as the man threw open the door and climbed into his vehicle. The chief gave a quick salute before throwing his car into reverse and pulling out of the parking lot.

"So, Mrs. Jenkins, you can't think of anybody?" Riley pressed.

Mrs. Jenkins thought for a moment before answering. "Come to think of it, there is one man who might wish revenge."

"Care to elaborate?" Smith asked.

"Well, a man named Travers Johnson used to work under my husband when he ran a cattle business. Once he died, the job of foreman went to Travers. The only problem was that he was a very disappointing worker. Most of the time, he forgot what he was doing and entire jobs were left undone. After a while, I fired him. He rambled about a standing job offer down at the hotel. I would start there."

"Thank you, Mrs. Jenkins. You have been very helpful."

The Pagosa Springs Hotel was only a block down the main highway, so a quick car ride was all that was required to get there. Upon entering, Detective Smith noticed that a man with dark-brown hair and a rugged face was doing paperwork.

"Excuse me, sir, do you know where we may find a Mr. Travers Johnson?"

"You found 'im. What can I do for you?"

"We are investigating the robbery of Mrs. Jenkins's purse, and we happen to know that you and her didn't exactly get along," Riley said.

"Hey, don't accuse me of nothing! Just because I was wandering around her place that night doesn't mean that I stole it!"

"You were what?" Riley countered.

"I...Well, you see... Fine, you got me. Jobs have been hard to come by lately, so when a man calls you out of the blue and tells you to snoop around a house, and that he will pay you well for it, you do it," Travers confessed. "Shouldn't have even done it, though. Guy told me to call a number when the job was done and he'd leave the money at the gas station nearest Jenkins's house. I called, told him what he wanted to know, and waited for the money. It never came."

"Do you by chance still happen to have that phone number?" Smith asked. Travers nodded, pulled out his phone, and handed it to the detective.

"Should be in there. Call came at around nine-thirty."

"Detective, a quick sidebar?" Riley asked. Smith walked with his assistant until they were well out of hearing range. "I don't trust this guy. He just happens to have the phone on him? Nope, I'm not buying his story. For all we know, he could have done it and made up the whole call thing to throw us off track. Here, I'll take the phone and deal with it while you investigate actual leads," he said.

"I do believe that I will hold onto the phone for now. Whether Mr. Johnson is trustworthy or not is out of the question. We still need to follow any lead available, no matter where it comes from," Smith commented back. He walked up to Travers once more and thanked him for the new information. As Smith turned to leave, he got a glance at the far side window of the hotel. The sign read: Handbags, Jewelry, All Things Glamorous. A thought forced its way into his head as he gazed upon the rows of purses lined up in the window. He motioned for Riley to follow and jogged across the street and into the store. It was evident that this was the place that sold Mrs. Jenkins her purse. Everywhere Smith looked, gems and bejeweled accessories shined out at him.

"Man, this glow might just be permanently imprinted into my vision," Riley grumbled somewhere to the detective's right. Smith ignored him and walked up to the front counter.

"My name is Detective Smith. Do you mind if I ask you a few questions?"

"Shoot," the woman behind the counter responded.

"Do you have recollection of a hundred-thousand-dollar purse that was sold to a Mrs. Jenkins?" Smith asked.

"Hard to forget something that expensive. But yeah, I do."

"Wait, something that costly would have to be insured, wouldn't it?" Riley cut in.

"Yeah, it would. In fact, I spent awhile helping her with the paperwork. Had to order that purse specially."

"Thank you for your time," Smith said. Riley seemed anxious to leave and was already out the door before Smith concluded his closing statement. The detective trailed his assistant and found him standing casually on the sidewalk.

"Detective, you don't think that she stole her own purse to get the owner's insurance, do you?"

"The facts are highly in favor of that opinion."

"Well, it would explain why she left her purse at home. She has to know how much it costs if it was ordered specifically for her," Riley commented.

"Exactly." Both men were silent as they thought about the possibility of this theory.

"Hey, Detective, you want to go grab a bite to eat? Crime solving sure does make you hungry," Riley suggested.

"No, thank you, there is one point of interest that I wish to explore."

Riley just shrugged and left Smith with his thoughts. Once Riley was gone, Smith hopped back into his vehicle and returned once more to the house of Mrs. Jenkins.

Mrs. Jenkins answered the doorbell within a few seconds of Smith's summons.

"I hate to intrude on any more of your time, but this cannot wait," Smith began.

"Detective, whatever do you want?" Mrs. Jenkins questioned. Smith could not help but note the exhaustion in her voice. Her dress, however, consisted of the same caliber of fashion as before.

"Mrs. Jenkins, I happen to have at my disposal the knowledge that you took out owner's insurance on your stolen purse."

"Yes, in fact, I did. But how does that..." She froze as the implications of her words sunk in.

"I do not believe that you carried out theft against your own purse, Mrs. Jenkins. I believe very strongly that there is another party involved. Does your house have an infestation of any kind, Mrs. Jenkins?" The sudden shift in topic caused Mrs. Jenkins to look at Smith as if something was wrong in his head.

"Termites. The fumigation company was supposed to have already cleared my house, but when I asked them, all they said was that they had 'been excused by authorities for inspection of the house.' Well, I went and asked the authorities, and they denied any such involvement in my house," Mrs. Jenkins spoke angrily.

"That is very interesting, Mrs. Jenkins," Detective Smith said slowly. The detective quickly said his goodbye and drove to the nearby park. The process of clearing his head and deconstructing the case was his usual procedure when all the cards were on the table. Smith's thoughts seemed to form on their own accord.

Travers Johnson. Mrs. Jenkins. Both are players in this game, but in what way? My instinct tells me that Mr. Johnson is truthful when he speaks about a mysterious man paying him to spy on Mrs. Jenkins's house. If this hypothesis is true, then the man who paid the ex-cattle rancher is the true culprit. Next is the peculiar story of Mrs. Jenkins. Does this story fit into my working hypothesis? Assuming that it does, then the same person who excused the workmen is the same as the one who phoned Mr. Johnson. This hypothesis, if true, effectively eliminates both Travers Johnson and Mrs. Jenkins from the equation. Who else is involved that could be the true suspect? Ah, the caller of course. I do believe it is high time that I take a look at that phone. He flipped open Traver's cellular device and scanned down the recent call list until he came across one with a time stamp of nine-thirty. The number before him shocked him to the core. In the blink of an eye, Smith unsheathed his own cell phone and navigated to his contacts. Both sets were an identical match. The more he desired it to be false, the more sense it seemed to make. With unsteady feet, Detective Smith stood up and set a course for the hotel suite of Riley Stevens.

Riley was settled in deep thought with his back to the door when Smith walked in. Riley started at the sound of the door closing.

"Oh, Detective. I didn't see you come in. Have you found anything else out about the case?"

Instead of answering verbally, Smith seized the notepad that was on the nearby nightstand and quickly flipped through it. A slight tear could be seen at the top of a page somewhere in the middle. The incriminating evidence shined up at Smith like a diamond. The numbers 294852 were dully printed on the page below where the thick ink pen had bled from the page above. Riley's face slowly fell as comprehension dawned on him.

"Why did you do it, Riley?" Smith asked his most trusted friend.

"I guess you know all about it then."

"I believed that I knew you better, but I guess every human has a weakness."

"Tell me, great and powerful Detective Smith, how exactly did I do it?" Riley shot back sarcastically.

"It was simplicity itself for you to become Mrs. Jenkins's friend. Given the amount of time that you possessed and the thought that you were there to help her, Mrs. Jenkins put everything into your hands, even the code to her alarm system, if I am not mistaken. She told you about the purse, and you couldn't resist. You called Mr. Travers Johnson to scope out the house, and you knew about the owner's insurance, providing the perfect red herring for your crime. Unfortunately, it slipped your mind to erase the data of the phone call from Mr. Johnson's phone. Mrs. Jenkins would never have guessed that the person she trusted most was the person she should have trusted the least."

Riley Stevens leaned back in his chair and put his hands behind his head.

"Very impressive. Very impressive indeed! Well, Detective Smith, what are you going to do with me now? Are you going to call the police?" Riley taunted.

Smith said nothing. He looked at his best friend with eyes full of sadness.

"Well, this has been fun, but I do think that I have a flight to catch," Riley said.

Riley Stevens shoved Smith out of the way and threw open the door only to be face to face with the county sheriff. He slowly began to nod as he turned to face his accuser.

"You are too smart for your own good, Detective Smith! Have you even thought about how others think when compared with you? Just once, I wanted to pull the wool over your eyes and make a pretty penny in the process. But you always have to end up on top, don't you?" Riley was screaming.

With those words. Riley Stevens stormed out of the hotel suite led by the sheriff. Smith stood looking after his assistant for a few moments, then walked out of the suite, and closed the door. He drove straight from there to the airport where he got on a flight headed for home. Never once did Detective Smith look back.

THE BRIEFCASE

The Second Adventure Recorded By Detective Smith

THE MAN IN BLACK

The storm clouds blocked out the moon as the man made his way through the deserted street. If you were a passerby and happened to look his way, you would see nothing. For this man was on a mission—a mission that required stealth and cunning. Dressed in all black from head to toe and practically invisible in the darkness of the night, he started to jog. As he turned a corner, he felt the cold cylinder inside his pocket hit his leg. *Only if I have to*, the man thought to himself. Lightning flashed and, for a moment, lit up the face of the unknown man. He saw himself reflected in one of the windows of a passing house and grinned. The man had no distinguishing features, aside from a strong jaw and large cheekbones. He could have blended into any crowd that he so desired.

He came to a stop at the street sign. Looking to his left, then to the right, he made a break for the abandoned shed on the far side of the street. Not a light on the whole street was turned on.

Better to cover my tracks.

Just as he was about to continue on his quest, the street was suddenly as bright as if it was broad daylight. He ducked behind a Dumpster to avoid the car's glare. *Just go on by*, the man pleaded to the silent night. But no such luck. The car stopped, and out came a plump little man.

"I know you're here," the man said in a quivering voice. He shakily pulled out his cell phone and hurriedly clicked three buttons. "Hello, I just saw a shadow that looked like a man move in the darkness and I think that you should send an officer here right away!"

The man in black reached for his pocket but stopped halfway once the conversation dissolved into whispers. Instead, he picked up a rock and threw it as far as he could away from himself. With a loud bang, it hit a parked car at the far side of the street. The plump man jumped and pulled out a can of pepper spray while converging on the noise. The man in black blew a sigh of relief and slipped from his hiding spot. He hurriedly went in to the abandoned shed and shut the door. Turning on the lights revealed a sad scene. The whole place was falling apart. Furniture was turned over itself and strewn across the room; the stairs leading to the upper floors were barely holding together.

"There you are," said a deep voice. From what appeared to be the kitchen entryway, another man appeared. But this man was the exact opposite of the one on the street trying to catch himself a pay raise by apprehending a criminal. This man was tall and skinny, with some muscle around his arms.

"Sorry, I was held up on the street," responded the man in black.

"No matter. Shall we do what we came here for?"

The man in black's heart rate picked up. "But of course. Just one question first. Why here, in this abandoned shed?"

The other man looked mildly amused. "Because this is the place no one suspects for a meeting to be held. This place has been condemned for months. No one would dare come in here."

"Makes sense."

The tall man grabbed something from behind him and pulled it out of the darkness. "I believe this is what you came for?"

"A briefcase?"

"What else would be suitable?" he said in a sharp voice.

The man in black could tell that he was somebody that would be easily angered. "Forgive me. I did not mean to doubt your abilities to get things where they need to be."

The man's expression softened. "Let us just be done with this." He sat the briefcase down on a nearby table and thrust it open. The light shined on the one million dollars that were lined up crisply in neat stacks.

"All of it is in here?" the man in black asked.

"Yes. All one million of it."

"But he doesn't suspect a thing, right?" the man in black said with some regret in his voice. He had been a little uneasy about what he had done.

"Not a thing."

A sigh of relief came from the man in black. "Good."

He moved to take the money, but the tall man's hand stopped him. "I have put a lot on the line for this, you know," he said.

"I realize that, and I thank you."

The tall man eyed the man in black. "You will give me half."

The man in black had been afraid of this. He figured that his agent would want some payment for his deeds. "I need this money. I am sorry, but I cannot afford to give up that much."

"I see. I was willing to negotiate, but you brought this on yourself," the tall man responded as he pulled from beneath his jacket a pistol and pointed it at the man in black. "I apologize for my actions." He pulled the trigger, but before it had time to go off, the man in black grabbed the tall man's hand holding the gun and pointed it at the light socket. The shot rang through the air as it connected with the man in black's intentions. They were plunged into total darkness. The man in black grabbed the cylinder in his pocket and thought, *This better be worth the time, tests, money, and effort I put into it!* He thrust the needle into the man's arm. With a muffled cry, the tall man crumpled to the ground. Without saying a word, the man in black grabbed the briefcase, headed out the door, and was lost once again to the night.

THE RETURN OF DETECTIVE SMITH

The chief inspector sighed heavily as he sat down his office phone. *Does it ever end?* he thought as he jotted down the address of his next crime scene. The chief had just finished a dead-end case involving a very big truck plowing its way into a jewelry store. That particular case had taken him four months to finally solve and put the criminal behind bars. But once again, he was being called into the field of battle. His police officer that was called to the scene did not elaborate much about what was going on. All he said was that something strange was happening, and he needed the chief right away. Chief Henry Bollard had never been one for mornings and did not have any particular inclination to investigate a crime in the beginning hours of one. With another sigh, he got out of his comfy office chair, grabbed his coat, and headed out the door. The chief was immediately hit with a blanket of cold rain. It had been raining ever since he went to bed and was supposed to continue into the following days. The chief hurriedly got into his car and drove off to the scene of his next battle. When he arrived, he noticed that a squad of his men were already on the scene and checking for evidence.

"What happened here?" the chief asked as he pulled one of the police officers from her duties.

She struggled to hear him over the wind and rain. "I can't explain much, Chief. You might want to go and ask Jefferson. He's the one who knows the most," she replied as she regained her umbrella from the clutches of the wind. The chief nodded and went inside the abandoned house. He shut the sad excuse for a door, and the wind died down at once. When he looked around, he realized with a grim expression that most of his men had trampled over everything that could have been evidence. This put his spirits down even more. He spotted Jefferson talking with someone who looked a lot like a reporter on the far side of the room. On his way there, he passed a frightened-looking officer who was interrogating a very tall, deep-voiced man. There was much yelling involved in the conversation, but the chief only had ears and eyes for one officer. He walked up to him just as the reporter left.

"I do not know how they know when there has been a crime. It's almost like they have a sixth sense or something," Jefferson complained with an exhausted voice.

"So, she is a reporter then?"

A sigh. "Yes."

"Great. What would we do without reporters breathing down our necks?" the chief asked sarcastically.

"Get the job done a lot faster, that's for sure," Jefferson said. The chief decided to turn things to the problem at hand.

"So what happened here?"

"That's just the thing. We have no idea. We got a call to the station saying that there was a body with a gun beside it, but when we got here, nothing. All that was here was the tall man over there." He pointed to the deep-voiced man talking to the shaking officer.

"Then why is everybody here?" the chief asked bluntly.

"The call we got was from a man who said that he chased the crook down on foot with a can of pepper spray late in the night."

The chief was getting impatient. "And how does that relate to us?"

"Ya know the drill, Chief. If somebody calls, we have to send an officer out there to check it out."

"But that still doesn't explain…" The chief stopped midsentence. What he saw drove all of the nonsense about this scene out of his mind. He walked over to the far wall, leaving Jefferson standing there with a confused look on his face. "Jefferson."

"Yes, sir?" he said walking over.

Jefferson's boss pointed to a spot on the wall. "What does that look like to you?"

"Why it…it looks like a bullet hole!" And so it was. There was a bullet hole straight into the wires of the light switch. "What do we do, sir?"

"There isn't enough evidence for an official investigation," the chief said, his mind working so quickly you could practically hear the thoughts forming themselves into ideas.

"Then how will we catch whoever did this?" Jefferson replied slowly as the chief turned his back to him and took out his cell phone. "Who are you callin', Chief?"

"An old friend," the chief answered.

Detective Smith drove up to the abandoned shed, his thoughts attempting to decide what would cause his old friend to call him here, at this hour. The rain, now accompanied by numerous flashes of lightening, picked up even more as the detective entered the house. Heads turned as he attempted to dry off in the entryway. Smith spotted his reason for being here in deep conversation with one of his employer's officers. Judging by his demeanor, he was a higher-up in the organization. But the minute he entered, the chief stopped his conversation and made his way over.

"Detective Smith, it is truly an honor to be working with you again," the chief said enthusiastically, shaking the detective's hand.

"Likewise, Chief. And I believe congratulations are in order for completing another difficult case," Smith replied. "I saw it in the paper," he added in answer to the chief's questioning looks.

"Thank you, Detective. That case was a particularly long one."

"Have you had any other cases since we last met?"

"Nothing major. Just the one."

"So what occasion has brought us both here today?" Smith asked, instantly changing from pleasure to business.

"I can't make heads or tails of it," the chief said, all the day's troubles coming out of him in one breath.

"Then, I might be of assistance. What happened here?"

The chief breathed a sigh of relief. Finally, glad that someone was here with whom he could thoroughly rely, he explained the problem at hand. "I've gotten all my information from Jefferson, so this comes not from my observations, but his."

"And Jefferson is your deputy, correct?"

The chief gave a puzzled look. "How did you know that?" he asked.

"I noticed when I first came in that he holds himself up with, what I took, to be pride. Pride coming from a recent promotion would be the only explanation. And the way he gives orders to other officers when you are busy suggests that you are his only superior, thus making him your deputy," Smith explained. The chief's expression of question soon became one of admiration. After a moment's pause, he gave a laugh. "I knew I picked the right person! Who else could have figured that out in that little time?"

"No need to give me so much credit. With a few simple observations, a bigger picture can emerge," Smith told the chief while waving away his compliment.

"But still, Detective. That's mighty impressive."

"Why, thank you, Chief. It is always good to have someone else notice the small gifts that we all contain. But back to the problem that needs our immediate attention. Did Jefferson give you any clues that could help us with this case?" Smith asked.

"Nothing that I found revealing, but I will tell them nonetheless. When the station got the call, a young man's voice told the operator that there was suspicious activity in this area. He then proceeded to tell the operator that he heard a noise and that he was going to investigate. Ignoring all the officer's warnings, the man proceeded to converge on the sound with a can of pepper spray. The station didn't think much of it until they got another call about three hours later by the same man. But this time, it held a different message. He said that there was a body in a rundown house with a gun beside it. So naturally, they sent a squad over to check things out. But when they got here, all they found was that very tall man over there." The chief pointed to the man who was now getting very angry at the pale, quivering officer. "But there was no gun in sight nor the 911 caller. And those are the facts, Detective," the chief concluded.

Smith was deep in thought. "Did the caller give any description of the body?"

"No, he said that everything was dark and that he couldn't see well."

"Hmm. So what was a mysterious man doing in a pitch-black house where a body should have been?"

The chief opened his mouth to reply, but just then, Jefferson came to the duo.

"Hey, Chief. Just thought you might want to know..." Jefferson stopped midsentence, noticing who the third party was. "No way... Detective Smith?" As Smith nodded, Jefferson continued, "I can not believe this! You are my hero! All of your cases have reached the ears of all of us down at the station. We cannot believe the skill you show in solving cases. Truly awe inspiring." Jefferson beamed as he shook the detective's hand.

"That is very kind of you to say, Mr.?"

"Trueman, sir," Jefferson answered instantly.

"Ah yes. Thank you. The chief here has just informed us on your observations, Officer Trueman," Smith told the young man in front of him.

"A very confusing case. But now that you are here, things should go smoothly," Jefferson said, barely concealing the excitement in his voice.

"What are your takes on the matter?" Smith asked.

Jefferson's eyes shone. Eager to prove his worth to this famous detective, he answered, "At first, I thought it was just another false report. Until I saw the bullet hole, that is."

"Bullet hole?" the detective questioned, his interest finally set on fire.

"You didn't tell him, Chief?" Jefferson looked at the chief.

The chief seemed caught off guard. "I was going to show him after he was caught up on previous events. But then you came in, so I thought that you could show the good detective."

Jefferson's expression got even more joyous. "It would be my pleasure, Chief. Right this way, Detective." Jefferson led the way to the light switch closely followed by Smith. They passed the tall man and the officer who were now yelling at the top of their lungs to each other. The chief motioned for them to go on as he stepped in to intervene between the two before it got violent. Jefferson shrugged at Smith and continued on to the spot where their case got more interesting.

"Here it is, sir."

Detective Smith took a moment to look at the point where the bullet entered.

"You told the chief that the caller said that all was dark when he entered?" Smith asked Jefferson while quickly putting two and two together.

"Yes, sir, he did." Smith's eyes shone with a brightness that was not there before.

"Interesting. Very interesting," the detective said deep in thought. Jefferson was about to reply when the chief came over to them. He had obviously been doing a bit of yelling himself, for he was very red in the face.

"I can't get anything out of either of them!" the chief complained with a rough tone.

"Maybe I can be of assistance," Smith offered.

"Be my guest."

Smith walked over to where things were starting to get heated.

"*I already told you, I don't know*!" the tall man bellowed at the scrawny officer, making him, if possible, look even smaller. Smith decided this was a good time to jump into the fray.

"What seems to be the problem?" he addressed both of them.

"Who are you?" the tall man snapped at Smith.

"My name is Detective Smith. I was called to help with an ongoing investigation."

The man's eyes stopped glaring, but his tone did not let up. "Finally! Someone who looks like they can actually help! This weasel just makes things worse!" He thrust a long finger at the officer. The chief pulled the officer aside and whispered something in his ear. He looked relieved beyond belief and left the scene.

"Why don't you just tell me what's wrong, and I'll see if I can't help," Smith said in a soothing voice. Nothing was worse for an interrogation than for the person whom you are interrogating to be upset.

"All these people expect me to know everything," the tall man said. Smith decided that the best course of action was to turn things away from what would make this man angry, which came very easily.

"It's all right. What is your name?"

"Tom. Tom Verner."

"Well, Mr. Verner, do you know why you are here?" Smith asked carefully. It was imperative that he chose his words with caution. Tom sighed through gritted teeth. It was obvious that he was trying hard to not get angry at someone who was genuinely trying to help.

"No. I do not. Last thing I remember, I was getting ready for dinner last night. Then I find myself waking up on the floor of some unfamiliar building, and it is morning. And I spent the rest of my morning being yelled at by some cop!" Mr. Verner explained, his angry tone still present.

"Hmm, amnesia I would guess." Smith observed.

"But amnesia from what?" the chief asked.

"That is the question, my old friend."

The chief thought for a moment. "Well, I would say that he hit his head. What do you think, Detective?" But something had caught Detective Smith's attention to such a degree that he didn't hear the chief. His whole body had gone rigid and his gaze fixed itself on a singular area of the ground. "Detective?"

"Chief?" Smith questioned.

"Yes, Detective?"

Smith motioned to a spot on the floor. "Would you be so kind as to stand right there?"

The chief responded with a questioning look but did as told. Smith moved to where he was about five feet away from the chief. "Perfect. Now, if you do not mind, can you point a gun at me?"

The chief's expression got even more confused. "What's this all about Detective?"

"In good time, Chief. In good time," Smith answered, glancing to his left. In an instant, Smith grabbed the chief's hand and pointed it to the wall. "Something is not right, though…" Smith adjusted the chief's hand to where it was pointed about a foot above his head right at the light socket. Detective Smith gave one of his triumphant smiles. "Just as I thought."

"What's just as you thought?" the chief asked, his confusion mounting even higher.

"When the police station got a call, a man said that there was a body with a gun beside it. But he couldn't see because all was dark. I thought nothing of this matter until your very eccentric Jefferson showed me the bullet hole straight through the light switch. A shot like that would have taken out the lights," the detective explained.

"But why would someone want to take out the lights?" the chief asked. The chief's mind was very "on the problem now"—orientated that he had trouble wrapping his mind around this discovery.

"Exactly! That is why I think that the shooter had no intention of knocking out the lights," Smith told the trio.

"Hold the phone!" the chief said dramatically. "Why was there a shooter here in the middle of the night? And where did the gun go?" When the chief had said this, he had moved slightly to his left, exposing the telltale signs of the night before. Smith walked over to the small table that was in front of him.

"Aha!" Detective Smith said. All three of his audience drew blank stares. Smith started to elaborate. "If you happened to take a cursory look at this table, nothing but a lot of dust would meet your eyes. But if you took a closer look, you would notice a rectangle of dust that is lighter than the surrounding areas. I am not a professional in this department, but I would guess that it belongs to a briefcase."

"A meeting!" the chief blurted out. He smiled to himself, proud that he just solved a clue. Smith gave a reassuring nod. Jefferson was so impressed that he actually started to clap.

"But a meeting for what?" Verner asked slowly, obviously having a hard time understanding.

"That is the million-dollar question," Smith answered. All four of them sat in silence thinking about the flow of clues they just received. Jefferson turned to the detective. "So what now, sir?"

"I think that we have acquired all that we can from this place," Smith replied.

The chief nodded. "I agree. This place is starting to bring me down." And as if the world was proving his point, a loud clash of thunder echoed overhead.

Smith looked up at the roof. "We better hurry if we hope to catch this criminal," Smith remarked. Everyone nodded except Verner.

"Can I go now?" he asked.

The chief jumped at his voice. In his trance of thought, he forgot that Verner was there. "Go check with our paramedic, then you are free to go," the chief said as he pointed to an officer about to leave. Verner hurried to catch up to the officer about to face the torrents of rain pounding down. Once Verner left, the chief's cell phone rang.

Jefferson raised his eyebrows at this. "Really, boss? 'The Final Countdown'?" he asked in answer to his boss's ring tone. The chief waved him down as he walked away to take the call.

Smith turned to the smiling young man. "What do you think about this business?"

"Hmm, if there was a meeting, then that will give us two people involved. So if we can find one, then we might be able to find the other. The only problem is that if the item being given was stolen, then we have a very small margin to catch him," Jefferson said in one breath, clearly dying to give his take on the matter for a while.

"You are right on both points. I think our best course of action would be to try and find, if anything, the *something* that was stolen," he answered as the chief made his way back to the duo.

"It seems like every time we get into the thick of it, I have to leave," the chief commented, shaking his head.

Smith smiled remembering the last occasion that the chief was called away.

"Another truck through a jewelry store?" Smith asked, still chuckling to himself.

"Ha ha, not this time. I just got a call from the station. They think that they might have a suspect in another ongoing case," the chief replied.

Jefferson drew a deep sigh. "Let me go get my stuff then," he said in a downcast voice, sad that he was called away from the famous detective.

Smith gave him a pat on the back. "Don't worry about it. We will have plenty of opportunities to compare notes later."

"Really? You're serious?" Jefferson asked in a quivering voice.

"Of course. You have some smarts underneath that head of yours," Smith said.

"Wow. Th-thanks!" Jefferson sputtered out as he waddled away. The chief shook his head and muttered something like "crazy kid" under his breath. He turned and shook Detective Smith's hand. "Until next time, Detective."

"Keep an eye out for any clues, Chief. We need all the help we can get," Smith said. The chief inspector nodded as he turned to leave. Smith stood alone, taking one last look at the place that brought a very interesting case to his hands. He smiled to himself at the challenge that lay ahead of him as he turned the knob on the door and headed out into a hauntingly dark day.

THE CONNECTION

Detective Smith opened the door to his dark and quiet house with nothing but the day's recent events on his mind. He hung his keys on the hook and continued into the kitchen. Smith started making some coffee as he glanced at the clock. It read twelve o' clock noon.

All right, Smith thought to himself, *given the time that the crime was committed and the weather, I would guess we have about forty-eight hours to catch our man.*

He picked up his coffee and headed into his living room that was also his office. Sitting down in his chair, he took a sip of his drink and started to sift through all of the information that the day yielded.

First things first. We have a midnight meeting that took place in an abandoned house that was condemned, so the pair obviously did not fear detection.

Smith replayed his visit to the scene of this interesting crime in his head.

And the fact that the man who called the police was not injured or killed shows that one, or both, of the people involved were not willing to hurt somebody. But why did the 911 caller run after he called?

He made a mental note to come back to that later.

Then there is the light switch with the bullet hole in it.

Smith took a sip of his coffee.

Hmm, they must have had a falling out if guns were involved. And the fact that the light switch was shot suggests that it was not the original target. So one of the culprits would have to have a very quick reaction time to direct the bullet toward the socket. And the other would have to be a very exact height, assuming that the shot was fired straight.

Another sip. He had a strange feeling that there was something that he missed.

The briefcase.

Smith's thoughts were silent for a moment. He reached for a piece of paper and picked up his pen. With it he wrote:

1. the missing caller
2. the second man
3. the briefcase

Detective Smith looked at his three leads. Deciding that the chances of finding the missing caller and the second criminal were minimal in this torrential downpour, he stood up, downed the rest of his coffee, grabbed his coat, and headed out to follow the lead on the briefcase.

Driving in the flood that was coming from the sky was like trying to tame a very hungry and wild tiger, in Smith's opinion. A drive that would normally take about fifteen minutes was now taking about thirty. All the roads in town were deserted on account of the weather and the fact that it was Friday afternoon. Not even police cars could be spotted out in this condition. But Smith pressed on, determined to figure out as much as he could about the briefcase that was used in the mysterious meeting. His mind drifted to different avenues, and soon, he was lost in deep thought. But all of his thoughts were shattered when a car that was going way too fast, started to careen out of control. It spun out of its lane and flew into the opposite road. Since the visibility was horrendous, Smith did not see it until it was too late to stop. He grabbed the emergency break and jammed it up. The tires on his car screeched and stopped, turning his car sideways. But the wet asphalt made the car continue on its course. Seeing that this was futile, he tried a different tactic. Smith saw that the other car was going to hit him with its back, so he used that to his advantage. Turning the steering wheel as far as he could, he put the gas pedal as far down as it would go. This made his car face the opposite direction of the road he was on. Both cars slammed into each other with so much force that it blew both rear bumpers off and stopped both cars in their tracks.

Smith tensed all his muscles to make sure he was all right. A little bruised, but otherwise okay. A massive sheet of rain hit him in the face as he stepped out of his car. The car that caused Smith a hefty repair bill was no better than his. He ran over to where the car rested and pulled a man no older than himself out of the wreckage.

"Are you all right?" Smith asked the panting man.

"Yeah... Yeah, I'm all good. You?"

"Yes. What happened?"

The man looked at his car. "I was in a hurry to get home, and I must've hit something on the road." Smith looked up as lightening struck nearby.

"I say we get out of this weather before something worse happens," Smith suggested. The man nodded.

"I agree." They tested both cars and found that the detective's was the only one that still worked after the collision. Smith drove to a café in town, so they could wait out the weather. It was empty except for a rough-looking man drinking something that was suspiciously green.

The man led Smith to a corner table. "Thanks for the ride…"

"Detective Smith."

"Peter Connor," the man said as he took Smith's outstretched hand. In the light, the detective saw just how tired his café partner looked. His hair was standing out in all directions. It had what looked like gel in it as if he had tried to tame it but failed. He was wearing a battered-looking T-shirt that had a few holes in it and ripped jeans that were too short for him. "So you're a detective?"

"Yes, I am actually in the process of investigating a case right now," Smith said.

"Oh, really? What's it about?" Connor asked.

"Late last night, the police station got a call saying that there was a body lying on the ground of an abandoned shed with a gun beside it," Smith started to explain, "but when they got there, there was no gun or body anywhere to be found." Connor drew a look of confusion on his face.

"If nothing was there, then why were you called in?"

"Well, the chief inspector found a bullet hole straight through a light socket."

Connor's confusion mounted. "A light socket? But why?"

Smith did a flicking motion with his finger. "That is the main question."

"Hmm," Connor said thoughtfully.

"Indeed," Smith concurred.

"Well, what you guys need to do is find that gun," Connor said slowly. Smith gave him a thoughtful expression. "You've seen all those crime shows," Connor continued. "Once they find the gun, they find out who bought it, who sold it, etc., etc."

"That's a really good idea. I'll let the police know once my calendar is open," Smith said somewhat relieved. He was glad that somebody gave him a good lead. But at the mention of time, Connor jumped up and looked at his watch.

"Ah, crap! Sorry, Detective, but I have to go."

Detective Smith got up and shook Connor's hand. "It's been a pleasure, Mr. Connor. Thanks for the idea about the gun," Smith said.

"Oh yeah! About that, I have a friend who is in the Pagosa Springs Forensics Department. I can try to see if he can help you find the gun. And he can probably dust it for fingerprints if you find it."

"That's very generous of you, Mr. Connor. Up until now, I have never required the expertise of the Forensics Department and would be very grateful for any assistance. So, I think I will take you up on that offer," Smith said as he gave Connor his number. With a thank you, Peter Connor left the café and hailed a cab..

Detective Smith paid for their drinks and followed his new contact out in to the rain. An hour later, Smith drove home disappointed. The afternoon was already upon him and he had nothing to show for the time. He went to a locally known men's department store to try and hunt down the briefcase that was used in the midnight meeting. The owner of the establishment said that they hadn't sold any briefcases that matched the dimensions of the one that Smith described in a while. Their most recent sell was a month ago to an average-sized man of average height.

One down, two to go, Smith thought as he fought to make some headway in the tsunami falling from the clouds. The detective thought hard as to what his next move should be. He decided to investigate the identity of the man from the 911 call on the night of the crime.

This weather is too fierce to launch a full search, so I will have to go with the next best thing.

Smith pulled into the police department with one thing on his mind. The police HQ was the tallest building in town. Being four stories tall and with countless subdivisions and departments inside, it was very respectable. When Detective Smith was younger, it used to be a miniscule one-story building. Smith walked through the large, double glass doors into the main entryway. A few officers saluted him as he passed by.

"Ah, Detective Smith! Always a pleasure!" the receptionist welcomed Smith.

"Hello, Mrs. Clark. Do you know if the chief is in?" Smith asked.

"One moment. Let me check my computer," Mrs. Clark said as she turned and started typing rapidly. "No, I am afraid that the chief is away on business. May I take a message?"

"No need to trouble yourself," Smith answered as he turned to leave. "Actually, there is one thing."

"Name it."

"I'm investigating a particularly interesting case that happened last night, and I think it might be profitable if I could listen to the 911 call that was made."

"Anything for you, Detective. The recording room is on the third floor, second room to your right."

"Thank you. Have a nice day!" Smith called over his shoulder. He made his way up the elevator, to the room that the receptionist indicated. The recording room was full of computers and servers with a couple operators standing with their backs to Smith. One of them reached around to pick something up and noticed the detective.

"Detective Smith? What brings you to this part of the woods?" one of the operators asked excitedly.

"I would like to hear a recording, if that is fine with you."

"Of course! Out of all the times that you helped us, I'm sure that we can help you! Follow me over to where Dan is. I'm Frank Giles, in case you're wondering." The operator led the way to where another man was working. "Hey, Dan. The detective wants to listen to a recording."

"Well, recordings are our specialty!" the man named Dan exclaimed as he spread his arms out to indicate all the computers.

"It's all very impressive," Smith complimented to the operator. He smiled as if Smith had just complimented him.

"All these babies equal our pride and joy! They have been outfitted to hold all the recording and information that callers and tip givers give us," Dan started to explain.

"Sorry to cut in," interrupted the other operator. "Is there anything in particular that you want to hear? It takes a little while to locate a certain recording with everything coming and going."

"If it is not too much trouble, I would like to hear the recording from last night calling about a man inside a building," Smith explained. The operator got to work, trying to find the requested bit of tape. "So all these computers capture every singular recording that comes to the police station?" Smith asked Dan.

"That's right. These servers are hooked up to the phone lines, and whatever is said goes straight to the files in the hard drive."

"Impressive," Smith said, nodding his head.

"Thank you!" Dan said as his partner kept hammering away though files with different recordings. Smith got a glance of one about an attempted breakout from prison but didn't pay much notice. He was concentrating on the problem that had arisen within the last twenty-four hours.

"How exactly do you pull out a certain recording among others?"

"Well, first you have to locate which hard drive they're on. Usually, the most recent go into the one with the most space. So he will have to target which computer has the most space and then go into it and pick which recording fits the time frame," Dan explained.

"Got it!" Frank announced with enthusiasm. "What was my time?"

Dan looked at his watch. "Three minutes and fifteen seconds."

"Yes! Take that, Forensics Department! Who has the fastest analyst now?" he said, jumping out of his chair and pumping the air with his fist. "Oh yeah. Your recording. Uh, ah! Here it is." He pressed a button on his keyboard, and a woman's voice was heard.

"911. What's your emergency?"

"Hello, I just saw a shadow that looked like a man move in the darkness and I think that you should send an officer here right away!" a timid man's voice said.

"I'm sorry, but that isn't really an emergency."

"No, the shadow is by that condemned house. That's trespassing, right?"

"I'll send someone over there, sir."

"No, no! It might be too late! I'll go get him! I have some pepper spray in the glove compartment." It was evident that the man was trying to get credit for catching a criminal.

"Sir, don't go out there. It could be dangerous," the dispatcher warned. A loud bang issued from the timid man's end, and the line went dead. Dan cut the recording.

"That's all of this one, Detective. The man called back again a few minutes later. "Let me see…alright here is it." The 911 operator's words drifted once more through the air.

"911. What's your emergency?"

"Hi, I called you about five minutes ago about the trespasser? Well, I saw him go into the condemned house and decided to wait until he came out before I went in. I'm in there now and…oh my…is that a gun? Wha…is that a body?! I gotta get outta here!" the timid man screeched. A slight click signaled the end to the call.

"Could you go back toward the end where we heard that loud noise?" Detective Smith asked, thinking out every possible conclusion. The operator did as he was told.

"What do you guys think that is?"

"Could be metal hitting metal," Dan suggested.

"Maybe. But a more high-pitched clang would be heard if it was that," Smith said.

Dan looked a little hurt.

"How about lightening striking something close by? It was raining hard that night," the other operator proposed, eager to succeed where his colleague did not. Smith shook his head with a thoughtful expression.

"Can I get my own recording? I want to do a little digging." A few minutes later, Detective Smith was walking out of the HQ with yet another clue in his hand. He drove to the abandoned shed. He grabbed an umbrella and got out of his car. Thinking back to the recording, Smith figured that if the caller saw the man on the road, then he wasn't in the house yet. Imagining that the pepper spray toting man parked his car a few hundred yards away from the building, then the criminal would have to have been close by also. Smith thumbed the On button of his flashlight and looked around him. The only thing that could provide cover was an old Dumpster. The detective ducked behind it. He peered around the corner of the left side.

So the car's headlights would be shining on him while he was hiding.

Smith looked around him for anything that could cause a distraction. Behind him was rubble from the condemned house. He grabbed a rock from the pile and looked over the top of his hiding place. From here, Smith could see that the man that used this spot to avoid detection in the night had options. He could have thrown the rock at the man, most likely knocking him out and taking him out of the equation. Or he could have waited until he left, then continued on with his quest. But that bang on the recording told a different story. Smith stood up and threw the rock as hard as he could to his right. It hit something in the mass of rain and made a loud thud. Detective Smith smiled to himself.

The man had caused the loud noise by throwing a rock into the darkness. This made the timid man converge on that spot, allowing the other man to make a stealthy get away. But by throwing that rock, he provided a quick and easy diversion, showing that he had a secret appointment to keep, Smith's thoughts concluded. He tucked that clue into his mental pocket and got back inside his car.

Detective Smith sat down once again into his comfy, leather chair. He added his most recent clues to the steadily growing cluster of evidence that was at his disposal. But before he could get himself settled in, there was a knock on his door. Smith got up with excitement building. He hoped that the chief had came bearing good news about the case. When he opened the door, his hopes came crashing down. A young man, no older than thirty, was standing at his threshold, dripping wet. The detective invited him in and closed the door. In the light, Smith could see that his guest was looking very haggard. He motioned him into a nearby chair and took up his own post.

"I didn't know where else to turn. The police said to come to you because they were busy with an investigation," the young man said, looking at the trail of water he left behind him.

"Don't worry about it. That's one of the reasons I got tile," Smith assured, smiling to the man.

"I have a big problem. One that might possibly ruin my life."

"Big problems are my specialty. What can I help you with?"

"I should probably start at the beginning," the junior of the two men said. Detective Smith settled in to hear his visitor's narrative. "My name is Harrison Savage. I used to be very poor until I came upon a great job. Well, my real occupation is working at a bank, but I found a little side job that is very profitable. I find rundown, beat-up houses, fix them up, and then sell them. I am my own realtor, so I get one hundred percent of the profit. I have been doing this for about five years now and have accumulated quite the bundle. And since I work at a bank, I can make sure that my money is safe and sound. Well, until recently. I came across a pretty expensive house a year ago and decided to do what I do best. I fixed it up and ended up selling it for about three hundred thousand. Needless to say, I was pretty excited. I added up all the money that I have made over the years, and the grand total came to around one million dollars." Smith had to give a nod of approval at the large sum. "I didn't tell anybody about it because, well, you can guess why. I kept the money locked in a safe in my house so it would be secure. I thought about putting it in the bank, but too many people have access to it. Anyway, I went to bed last night feeling that all was right with the world. I make a habit every morning of going to check the safe and make sure that everything is okay. This morning when I went to check, it was gone," Savage finished.

"Gone?" Smith asked.

"Yes. Gone. I asked my neighbors to see if anybody had been by my house, and they said that no one had come by."

"So you think that it was stolen?"

"That is the only conceivable conclusion that I could find," Savage sighed in one breath, collapsing farther back into his chair.

"And no one knew about your very large sum that was hidden in your house?" Smith questioned.

"Yeah, but do you think that someone I know could have stolen it from me?"

"We can't rule anything out yet," Smith said, trying to calm down his client.

"But not many of my friends were in town this week. They are mostly all on vacation.

"Hmm. So you noticed that your money was missing this morning?"

"Yes. I went to check on it at six o'clock. Why?"

"The timing is very interesting," the detective said, his mind buzzing. Savage drew a look of dawning comprehension.

"There is one more thing, Detective. It might not be much, but lately, I have been seeing a tall, deep-voiced man wherever I go," Savage said slowly. This one comment pumped adrenaline straight into Smith's thoughts.

A tall, deep-voiced man…

His mind flashed back to the angry man that was being interrogated by one of the chief's officers.

Both incidents were not singular. They are both the same crime. They are connected.

ANOTHER LEAD BROKEN

After Mr. Savage had left, Detective Smith's mind rejoiced. His client's interesting happenings had finally given a positive outlook on the case. For the first time, he thought he was actually starting to shed some light on a few points. He looked back at the three leads that seemed to be written ages ago. Smith grabbed his pen and crossed out the clue about the briefcase. That had been a dead-end. But the detective decided that wasn't quite the big player in the case as he had originally thought. His guest had elaborated enough to convey that the briefcase used in the crime was not his own. Smith circled the lead labeled the second caller and wrote "Best friend of Harrison Savage?"

He underlined "best friend" and drew an arrow to the newly written "Acquaintance with Mr. Verner." Underling this twice, he looked at the more exact lead. The only lead left was the missing caller. Smith decided to pick up where he left before his client appeared. The detective thought for a moment.

How am I going to locate a man based only on his voice? The police could track his cell phone, but that would take too long. We only have around forty-five hours left to catch our man. After that, any hopes of a solid, clear lead will be very difficult to land. The first forty-eight hours are indeed the most important in an investigation. Hmm.

Smith thought back to everything he knew about the mystery caller.

He was obviously driving home late at night, unless he was the one who committed the crime, then posed as a timid man to throw the police off his track. Either way, I need to find him. If he was trying to catch the criminal to get himself possible reward money, then he must work one of the lesser-paying jobs that might make him work the graveyard shift for more profit. Detective Smith did not even bother sitting down during his brain wave, knowing that he would be whisked away before he had time to relax. He looked around his moderate-sized home. With how much time that he spent away from his home dawning on him, a certain type of vigor gripped him as a new determination fought its way into the spotlight of Smith's feelings. Grabbing his umbrella, he delved back into the outside world to hunt down his first lead, the missing 911 caller/bounty hunter.

Detective Smith drove toward town thinking of all the jobs that he had come across in his life. He could think of none that had poor enough pay that someone would want to either steal money or get a bounty. He needed someone who had been around longer than himself. Taking out his phone, he dialed the chief's number. It rang for a couple minutes, then went to a voice mail. Smith put his phone in his pocket a little letdown.

Looks like I will have to do this the hard way, he thought with a sigh. In his mind, he eliminated half of the workplaces based on his experiences with clients. His thoughts came upon one in particular. It was only three in the afternoon, so the store would still be open, much to the favor of the detective. Smith entered into Jerry's Thrift Store with one thing on his mind. He went up to the front desk where a woman was working with her back to the detective. "Excuse me, but is Mr. Jerry around?"

"Sorry, hon, but he is out of town this week on business," the woman said, turning to Smith.

"What kind of business?"

"Just the usual when it comes to thrift store–type things, goin' to different places and tryin' to sell stuff. So we are a little shorthanded. But is there anything I can do for you?"

"I'm doing an ongoing investigation, and I would be very grateful if you could tell me how much you pay an hour," Smith said kindly.

"About nine."

"So would you say that your employees are generally happy working here?" Smith questioned. The woman thought for a second.

"Yes. I would say so. Why do you ask, hon?"

"I'm looking for a job that has a moderately low pay. An income so low that someone would resort to catching a criminal to get possible reward money."

"Heh. Sounds like the kinda thing someone working for McNab would do," the woman snorted.

"What is Mr. McNab's occupation?"

"He owns a construction business on the far side of town. Go down the main town rode for about five minutes, then turn off to the right and go a ways. Then you should see his building," the woman explained. The detective made a mental note of the directions.

"Thank you very much. Have a nice day!" Smith called as he closed the door to the thrift store. He made his way down the indicated rode and turned off where the woman had said. After a couple minutes, he passed by a very familiar site.

Looks like I'm in the right place, Smith thought as he drove by the condemned house that had been the center of his whole day. He came to a four-story building that was painted dark gray. He parked in the strangely empty parking lot and sprinted inside to avoid the unrelenting onslaught of pelting rain. The front office of the construction business was darkly lit and foreboding. A single man was relaxing in an office chair with his feet on the counter. Smith observed that his shoes were caked with a thick white film of dust.

"Excuse me sir, are you Mr. McNab?" Smith asked, walking up to the front of the desk. The man jumped at the detective's voice as he came out of his daze.

"Wha… Oh. Oh yeah. That's me. John McNab at your service," the man mumbled to Smith.

"I couldn't help but notice, where are all your employees?" Smith asked, a little confused at the owner's business ploy.

McNab's eyes narrowed to slits. "Are you one of those county commissioner guys?" McNab cautiously questioned, "I told them that I know what I am doing!"

"It's all right. I wasn't sent here by the county. My name is Detective Smith, and I need to ask you a few questions," Smith explained to the apprehensive owner.

This comment made McNab's eyes do the exact opposite of what they were.

"Why are you here? I didn't hurt anybody or do anything illegal. And if you are referring to that incident with the ice cream truck, I checked and there are no laws against that!"

"I'm not here for you. I need to locate someone that possibly works here," Smith said with an inward sigh. He could tell that this was going to be more difficult than was needed.

"Is it Ronald? I never liked Ronald…" McNab said eagerly.

"I believe that the man I am looking for is also on this recording," Smith explained while he took out the mini recorder that was given to him by the two enthusiastic operators. Smith laid it on the desk and pressed the Play button. For the second time today, the 911 operator's voice was audible through the miniature speakers:

"911. What's your emergency?"

"Hello, I just saw a shadow that looked like a man move in the darkness," the timid man's voice repeated.

"I'm sorry, but that isn't really an emergency."

"No, the shadow is by that condemned house. That's trespassing, right?"

"I'll send someone over there, sir."

"No, no! It might be too late! I'll go get him! I have some pepper spray in the glove compartment." Smith cut the recording and pocketed it once more.

McNab's eyes again turned to slits. "How dare he try and capture a criminal! I should have been there!

Heaven knows, I could use the reward money." Smith took this resentment as a good sign.

"I take it you know who this man is?"

"Yeah, I know him. Dale Harting is his name. Been working for me for the better part of five years. Always complains about the pay of the job, and he's always looking for some way to get more money. When I see him…" Smith could only catch a mumbling sound in substitute for the end of McNab's rambling.

"Do you know where I can find Mr. Harting?"

"I don't know. I sent all my employees home because of the possible flooding. No sense in keepin' everyone here when they can't work in this weather." Even though McNab was a little aggressive, Smith could tell that he knew what he was doing in ways of good management.

"Is there anyway that I can look at his address?" Smith asked politely.

"Why not? Let me grab his application real fast," McNab said as he disappeared into a back room. Smith heard a rustling noise, and then the owner came back into view. "Here you go." McNab slid the application across the desktop. Smith picked it up and looked inside the packet. What met his eyes was your typical application form. Average guy, worked a couple of odd jobs before finding the one that this application was for. No particularly noticeable achievements. At the bottom, Smith observed that Dale Harting had a black belt in karate.

That could account for the fast reflexes that one would need to have to redirect a gun, the detective thought to himself. He looked at the address, copied it to memory, slid the application back to McNab, and left the construction office with a hurried thank you.

Detective Smith knocked on the door of the small, cozy house that filled the space indicated to him on the application form. He heard footsteps from within the home, and a woman opened the door to him. "Hello, is Dale Harting in?" Smith asked nicely with a smile.

"No, I'm afraid he's not. May I take a message?" the woman said, returning the gesture.

"No, thank you, but do you know where I can find him?"

"He said something about going to the police department to straighten things out," she explained.

"Thank you. Can you tell your husband to contact me if I miss him, please?" Smith said, handing Mr. Harting's wife his phone number.

Mrs. Harting gave the detective a questioning glance.

"Your ring was the first clue. And if my nose is not deceiving me, that is meatloaf that I smell cooking. According to what you say, your husband left not too long ago because he was feeling uneasy about not telling the police he was the 911 caller. You most likely put on the meatloaf, not knowing that he was going to be somewhere, and so when he had to leave abruptly, you just left it in the oven," Smith explained.

"May I ask who you are?" the woman asked.

"My name is Detective Smith, and I'm investigating a case that your husband might be involved in,"

"Do you think he's guilty of something?"

"If he went to the police HQ to make amends, then I have strong feelings against it," Smith reassured the young woman. She let out a sigh of relief.

"I'm glad that you are on the case, Detective. I have heard of some of your cases in the past. Knowing that you think my husband is innocent is very good to hear," Mrs. Harting offered.

Detective Smith smiled to the woman in front of him. "My job is not just finding out who the criminal is, Mrs. Harting. It is also proving the innocent to be just that," he said as he turned to leave.

Smith pulled into the police HQ with a good feeling in his heart. He was about to uncover more information on this very puzzling case. The receptionist waved the detective in as he walked through the glass doors.

"You're just in time, Detective. Some man came in and requested to speak with the chief. He said his name was Dale Harting. His voice sounded very familiar and only when he left did I make the connection. He is the missing 911 caller!" the receptionist explained.

"Say no more. Where is the chief now?"

The woman pointed toward an office on the far side of the right wall. Detective Smith nodded and walked into the chief's office. He entered into a large chamber that had a decorative wooden desk on the far side. Behind this desk sat the chief. He was so listening intently to Dale Harting's story that he hadn't noticed when Smith walked in. The chief's deputy was standing against the wall, watching his boss. He saw the detective, and his face lit up. He fast walked over and shook Smith's hand energetically.

"It's an honor to see you again, Detective!" Jefferson said with a smile.

"The pleasure is all mine. So this is Mr. Harting?" Smith asked.

"Yes, sir. That's him. He got here around fifteen minutes before you did," Jefferson explained.

"Has he said anything that could incriminate him or wipe the suspicions from our minds?"

"Not yet. He has mostly been talking about his life in general: his wife, his job, and his boss. He just now got to the part we're interested in."

"Thank you, Officer Trueman. Let's see what we can learn from Mr. Harting, shall we?" Smith said as he led the way toward the chief.

"So let me get this straight," the chief began to say when he noticed the detective. The man in front of him was practically not there for a moment. The chief got up, walked around the man standing opposite of his desk, and shook Smith's hand. It was obvious that the chief was glad the detective was in his office. "I'm glad you're here, Detective. Me and Jefferson here had just closed a case when Harting here came in to my office," the chief said, jerking his head to the man standing in between the trio. "I should probably fill you in."

"No need, chief. I've been doing a bit of digging myself, and I can confidently say that I know a great deal about Mr. Harting here," Smith said.

The chief started to laugh. "I should have known that you wouldn't stay idle during this. You probably know more about this man than either Jefferson or me, so I will let you take the helm."

When the chief stepped aside, Smith got his first good look at Mr. Harting. He was nothing like his voice sounded on the 911 tape. He was of average height and build and wore an oxford shirt and tie.

"Like I have been telling the chief here, I am completely innocent," Mr. Harting started to explain. Detective Smith stopped him before he could waste any more breath.

"I completely believe that, Mr. Harting."

"You do?" It was apparent that he had come with a speech in mind.

"Yes, sir, I do. You have a kind wife who is willing to cook for you and who is willing to let you go and settle things that are bothering you. Your boss is aggressive, probably not just toward you but also to everyone. And I can vouch for that. It would not make sense for you to go and steal a large sum of money that would put your life in jeopardy," Smith reassured the second Harting in a time span of thirty minutes. Mr. Harting was completely caught of guard.

"How do you know so much about me?"

"I have talked personally to your boss and to your wife. But a couple points remain unanswered. Why were you coming home so late that night?" Smith questioned, pulling up the list of questions that he had filed in his mind.

"As you know, working for Mr. McNab is not a very high-paying job. There was some extra work that needed to be done around the building, so I stayed to do it."

"Can anybody confirm that?" the chief interrupted.

"Actually, yes." Mr. Harting said, turning to the chief. "A buddy of mine stayed to work also. Here's his number." Mr. Harting gave the chief a slip of paper, who, in turn, gave it to Jefferson.

"Check his alibi, Jefferson. If anything suspicious comes up, let me know," the chief whispered to Jefferson.

"You got it, chief," Jefferson said, taking his job with enthusiasm. When Jefferson left, Smith picked up where he had left off.

"Why did you call the police and then not stay to see things through?"

"I figured that since I disobeyed them, the police would not be too happy with me about leaving the scene of the crime," Mr. Harting said, embarrassed.

"It still was not the best thing to do. It makes you look like the bad guy. But since you came back to explain things, everything should work out." Smith could see the anxiety flow out of his face. "Would you please explain what you saw when you entered the condemned house?"

"After I chased down the trespasser and found nothing, I went into the abandoned shed thinking that whoever was outside might have come inside. It was pitch-black. I could barely even make out where I was stepping. Once my eyes got a little adjusted, I saw a body lying on the rusted tiles," he told the detective.

"What did this body look like?" Smith questioned, already knowing the answer.

"The body was that of a really tall man. He was a little muscular but nothing too impressive."

"Was there anything strange about the body?" the chief asked. Clearly, he was having a hard time staying out of the interrogation.

"Nothing too strange. Just looked like he had dropped right where he stood. Wait. He did have a strange marking on his arm though," Mr. Harting revealed.

"A strange marking?" Smith asked.

"Yeah. I got out my flashlight to investigate and found a small, little, dark-red mark on his arm. It looked like someone had gotten a pen and stabbed him with it. After I saw it, I decided to get out of there. I figured the police would be close behind me," Mr. Harting concluded. Smith looked at the chief whose expression was as confused as his own. Clearly, the marking was new information to the both of them. Just then, Jefferson walked back into the office.

"Everything checks out, Chief," Jefferson said. "He confirmed that he was working late that night with Mr. Harting."

"Thanks, Jefferson," the chief acknowledged. Smith was deep in thought.

"Mr. Harting, is there anyway that you could recreate that marking on the body that you saw?" Smith asked. Jefferson looked confused and was about to say something when the chief whispered something that sounded like "later" in his ear.

"Yeah, probably. It was pretty unique. Shouldn't be too difficult."

"I am going to need you to recreate that, if you can. It might just be the link we are looking for," Smith said as he handed Mr. Harting a notepad from his back pocket.

The chief looked a little surprised at this. "That's funny, Detective. All this time I have known you, I have never seen you pull out a notepad once on a case. Do you always carry it around with you?"

"Usually. I don't normally need it, but for things like this, it helps to have it with you," Smith explained. The chief nodded his appreciation. Mr. Harting scrunched his brows together in an attempt to remember the strange marking he saw that night. In the meantime, the chief whispered everything that had gone on in Jefferson's absence in his deputy's ear. There were a few puzzled looks, but in the end, comprehension took over.

"There! That's as best as I can remember it," Mr. Harting said, giving the notepad back to the detective. Smith stared at the marking, thinking hard.

"What is it?" Jefferson asked eagerly. Smith passed the drawing on to him. This yielded the same expression.

"It looks like he was stabbed with a really skinny blade. Maybe a fencing sword?" Jefferson handed it off to the chief.

"Could be, Jefferson. But it seems like it is something smaller," the chief remarked. Detective Smith remembered a conversation he had with Peter Connor, who just happened to have a friend in the Forensics Department.

"I know someone who has a friend in the Forensics Department. I'll send it his way and see what we can find out about it," Smith concluded. Jefferson's admiration increased at this comment.

"I don't mean to interrupt, but can I go? My wife does have meatloaf on, and nothing is worse than cold meatloaf," Mr. Harting said. All three of them nodded at the remark about cold meatloaf. Once again, the chief forgot about Mr. Harting being there in his trance.

"Yes, you can go. Thank you for your help, Mr. Harting," the chief said. Once again, it was just the three of them alone against a challenging case. The chief turned to Detective Smith and said, "If you don't mind me asking, Detective, can you fill us in? Jefferson and I really haven't had time to work on this case."

"Of course, Chief. After we left the condemned house, I thought about everything that I had seen and heard. I came up with three main clues: the briefcase, the second man involved, and the missing caller. We have just witnessed the missing caller, and it gave us a valuable clue. As for the briefcase, not so much. I checked and the briefcase was not bought anywhere in town, so it must have been his own. Not much to gain from that, but it still is something. And a man came to my doorstep asking for me. Apparently, his one million dollars was stolen from a completely secure safe that he kept in his house. No one knew about the money and its whereabouts. He is almost positive that a stranger stole it, but I think that it is worth checking out. Also, Mr. Savage noticed a tall, deep-voiced man following him throughout the past week," Smith explained.

"The two are connected," the chief said.

"Exactly. So the highlight of our case is that one million dollars was stolen from a safe and whisked away."

Jefferson whistled at the detective's summary. "If Mr. Verner is involved, then let's go ask him a few questions," Jefferson said.

"As much as I think that he is involved, I am almost certain we can get nothing from him," Smith remarked.

"Do you think that his story about not remembering a thing is real?"

"I do. I could see truth in his eyes. And when we walked up and tried to calm the situation down, he seemed relaxed. If he were part of it, his guard would have gone up, not down. Especially when the chief inspector, his deputy, and a detective walk over to him."

"But what's the possible link to his friends?" the chief threw in. He was eager to catch somebody and put him or her behind bars.

" Hmm, yes. We will have to do more work in that region. But if the perpetrator were the victim's friend, I doubt that he or she would need someone to follow him." All three of them sat in silence for a moment, thinking about the unsolved clues, and endless rabbit trails that still awaited them.

"Is there anything that we can do, Detective?" the chief asked.

Smith looked at him thoughtfully. "See what you can dig up about Verner's friends. It might go a long way in solving this case."

"Until next time, sir," Jefferson said as he shook Smith's hand and followed his commanding officer out. The detective stood in silence for a moment, thinking about the strange drawing in his hand. Smith ruled out a knife wound. A knife wouldn't cause amnesia. The fact that there was no blood rules out any kind of blade. Smith walked out of the chief's office, waved good-bye to the receptionist, and headed back into the rain and reached for his cell phone.

"Mr. Connor? Yes, it's Detective Smith. What was your friend's number again? No, we haven't found the gun, but I think that we have stumbled across something a little more interesting. That's why I want to call up your friend. 555-8760? All right. Uh-huh. Thanks again." Detective Smith was about to figure out what could possibly be the most important link in the investigation.

A CHANGE IN PERSPECTIVE

For the third time that day, Detective Smith found himself pulling into the parking lot of the Police Department. But unlike his previous visits, he was not heading toward the main structure. The Forensics Department was built on after the fact to house everything in a singular place. It was a small little building that looked as if it had fallen behind the modern style. Smith parked his car and headed toward the rundown building. He opened the door and walked in. The detective was pleasantly surprised to see that two people were hard at work, regardless of the nearing evening.

"I know, I know. It's a little messy, but we are waiting on the new building, so just bear with us," a man said without looking up from his work. "Hey, Maggie, can you pass that my way when you're done? Thanks." Once Smith's eyes adjusted to the dark lighting, he saw what the worker was talking about. Equipment was anywhere and everywhere that had space to put things. He walked up to the man that had his back turned to him.

"Hi, I'm Detective Smith. Do you happen to know where I can find a man by the name of Bernard? Peter Connor gave me his number and said if there was anything that I needed help with in the area of forensics, he was the one to see," Smith explained.

"Peter Connor, eh? Yeah, I know him. Good guy. So what do you need help with, Detective? I'm Bernard, by the way," the forensics expert said, turning around to face Smith. He was wearing glasses and had one of those faces that you immediately associate with scientific experiments. Smith took out the recently drawn picture of the strange marking on the victim's arm and handed it to Bernard.

"A witness in an ongoing investigation said that he saw a body with this strange marking on it. No one, including myself, could identify what it might be. That's why I need you," Smith explained.

Bernard looked closely at the drawing, thinking. "A very peculiar mark... Maggie take a look at this, and see what you think." The woman who was working beside Bernard took a look at the drawing.

"Hmm, it is interesting. None of the typical weapons apply here. I'm guessing that the person found on the ground was killed by this device?" Maggie asked the detective.

"Actually, quite the opposite. The man couldn't remember what happened in the past twelve hours, but otherwise, he was okay." The forensics duo both drew thoughtful expressions.

"Wait... I have an idea," Maggie said.

"I'm all ears," Smith responded.

"Before you came in, I was working on an easier way to inject someone with medicine. A hospital wanted me to fix a problem they were having with patients. Anyway, I did a lot of playing around with needles for the experiments. I got my hands on some test dummies from the hospital that hired me, so I could see if what I was doing looked more or less painful. A bunch of different results came out of it, but I eventually came across one injection system that didn't seem as painful as the rest. And the mark for said needle looked exactly like this," Maggie concluded.

The dam in the detective's mind broke, flooding his brain with thoughts.

The second culprit was playing with syringes. He settled upon the one that would hurt less, not more. On top of that, whatever he injected Mr. Verner with caused his amnesia, making it so that Mr. Verner couldn't give a testimony against him! He was concentrated on acquiring the money, not hurting anybody. That is why he went out of his way to make sure every aspect of his plan did not involve affecting anybody directly. Meaning that…

"He is a doctor," Smith exclaimed, all his thoughts coming to a head in a matter of seconds.

"That sounds about right," Bernard said.

"Do either of you two know any doctors that have been experimenting on needles?" Smith asked the duo. They both looked at each other and shook their head.

"Not that I know of," Maggie answered.

"Nope," concurred Bernard.

"Thank you for the information. Your help has been invaluable either way," Smith told them as he shook their hands goodbye.

"Good luck on the case, Detective!" Maggie called as Detective Smith turned the knob of the rundown Forensics Department and headed back into the driving sheets of rain. Smith got into his car, picked up his phone, and dialed the chief's number. "Hey, Chief, it's Detective Smith… Actually, I have a question. Do you know of any doctors in town that are experimenting with a way to make injections less painful? Our criminal just so happens to be one… That's exactly what I was thinking… Yes… Right you are, Chief… So do you know of any? Hmm. All right. Would it any trouble for you to meet me there? It wouldn't? Thanks, Chief… See you there." Smith hung up his end and headed to the new location given by the chief.

There were three main hospitals in town: St. John's, which was closest to downtown; Red Cross, which was on the outskirts of town; and St. Paul's, which was somewhere in between. The place that the chief indicated was none of these. The hospital of whose front door Detective Smith was standing was not familiar to him. He took a quick look over the building and concluded that it must have been hastily built. It lacked the grandeur of the other hospitals in town and seemed to be a little rundown. It had few windows, so it gave the impression of being secluded. Add in the rain, and it looked like your classic haunted house. The chief drove up and met the detective at the front door.

"So this is it?" Smith said.

"Yes, this is it. A little gloomy, if you ask me," the chief responded.

"I agree. But is this the only hospital in town that has been testing injections?"

The chief nodded. "I remember seeing a case about a drug bust. Some guy was injecting himself with drugs. You know, the classic drug case. When asked where he got his needles, he gave the name of this place. On further look, the needles were different than ordinary needles. They had a spring system that injected the stuff in, then popped right back out in less than a second."

"Sounds efficient," Smith noted.

"Looked efficient," the chief said.

"Let's see if we can shed any light on our mystery doctor, shall we?" Smith said, leading the way toward the door.

"I'll be glad to get out of this rain, it's starting to bring me down," the chief said to the clouds as he followed the detective inside the hospital.

The inside matched the outside perfectly. The lighting was dark, as if the hospital was trying to cut back on their electricity bill by barely using electricity. There was a small waiting room to the right that was completely deserted. Magazines were all over the chairs and the small table that filled the place in between. Smith looked back at the chief who made a face that said, "What have we walked into?" The receptionist at the front desk seemed like she could think of a million other places she would rather be than stuck in an empty hospital. She regarded them with a blank expression when the duo walked up.

"How may I help you?" she asked with a tone that matched her expression.

"Do you know if any of your doctors are experimenting with a way to make injections less painful?"

"Look, I'm just a receptionist. I wouldn't know two things about what the doctors here do. If you have any questions, you can take them up with the manager."

"Where might we find your manager?" Smith asked in a polite voice.

"Keep going down the hall until you come to a dead-end. His door should be on the left," the receptionist answered, not giving them both a second thought.

"You can tell that she's paid well," the chief remarked after they had started to make their way down the hall.

"Based on the condition of this place, I don't think that they have very much money to spare," Smith said. He led the way down the hall until they found the dead-end that the receptionist indicated. They opened the door and went in. The inside was a direct contrast to the rest of the building. It took awhile for Smith's eyes to adjust to the change in lighting, but once they did, it was easy to see where all the money was going. The manager's office was lit up so much that it looked like he had harnessed a small pocket of the sun. All his furniture was extravagant. From Smith's experiences, he could tell that it was not cheap.

"Looks like we found out where all the money has gone," the chief said in an undertone. Before the detective could reply, the manager noticed them.

"What are you doing in my office?" he questioned. Detective Smith turned his gaze on to the man sitting behind the finished wood.

"Hello, my name is Detective Smith, and this is the chief inspector," Smith introduced, holding out his hand.

"What are a detective and a chief doing in my hospital? Am I in trouble?" the manager responded, shaking both the chief's and Smith's hand.

"Not in the least. We were just wondering if you have been experimenting with ways to make injections less painful," Smith said.

"Not to my knowledge. Why?" It was evident that the manager did not like people intruding upon his time.

"It is for an investigation that we are looking into," Smith explained.

"Now that I think about it, I do remember one of my employees saying something about syringes," the manager said.

"What is his name?" the chief asked. The manager looked at something on his desk.

"Let me see…Wilson Thompson. Just last week, I overheard him asking around if there were any springs he could borrow. I thought it was the weirdest thing. And if you are thinking about asking him yourself, don't bother. All of his personal info that he gave me, address, phone number, and whatnot is all wrong. I just found that out a few days ago," the manager concluded.

"Why would a doctor have a need for springs?" Smith asked.

"I don't know, aren't you the detective? You figure it out," the manager said in a rough tone. The chief gave a sideways look at the detective that said, "He's of no more use."

"Thank you for your time," Detective Smith said as he and the chief left the manager's office.

"Well, he wasn't very friendly," the chief remarked to Smith when they were back outside.

"At least, he was able to give us another clue," Smith said, thinking on the positive.

"I don't understand why a doctor who is trying to make stuff less painful would want springs. It just doesn't make sense."

"As of right now, I couldn't agree more. But everything will reveal itself eventually."

"So where to now?" the chief asked.

"Hmm, we know the name of our suspect, what his occupation is, and what he was working on. We need to get our hands on whatever syringes he had. I would conjecture that he made a prototype. Since he was concerned with making it as painless as possible, he would have wanted to get it right," Smith explained.

"But to get the prototype, we would need an address," the chief said.

Detective Smith thought for a moment. "What we need is to find where he lives," Smith said.

The chief looked confused. "Wouldn't he have wanted to put it some place else besides his house? That seems a bit too obvious."

"It might be the most obvious, but it is the place where it is most likely to be."

"I'm not following."

"Let me see what I can do to clear things up a little bit. This doctor wanted to make something in secret so that nobody would ever find it. His work would be the number one thing that would come in handy to make his secret syringes. If his work were so important to the process, then one would figure that the device would be hidden around his workplace. However, hiding something that important in your desk just would not do," Smith explained.

The chief nodded his head. "Ah, I see. So you think that he'd have the equipment at his house?" the chief asked.

"That is what I want to find out," Smith answered. The chief started to say something else, but his ring tone interrupted him.

"Hello, it's the chief. Really? Again? All right, I'll be down there in a minute... Thanks, Jefferson." The chief finished his short conversation and gave a sigh. "Turns out that the last suspect we nailed wasn't the right guy. I wish cases could just be a simple grab a guy and move on. But it looks like you're on your own again, Detective. Good luck!" the chief yelled over his shoulder as he made his way to his car. Smith watched him drive away and decided to follow suit. He took one last look at the rundown hospital, turned, and went to follow his next lead.

Detective Smith thought hard about how he was going to track down his number one suspect's house with knowing barely anything about him save for his name and occupation.

Knowing his occupation isn't going to help much considering that the hospital that he works at is barely known to the public. Hmm. The police station is busy with their current case, so they probably wouldn't have the resources necessary to find him. I could try and find the realtor, but that would be very time consuming. That's not keeping in mind the amount of realtors there are.

A loud crash of thunder followed by a bright flash of lighting broke through Smith's thoughts and senses. If anything, the rain had picked up since he was inside the hospital. An idea hit Smith just like the display of nature that he just witnessed.

If he has lived here awhile, then his name should be in the town directory along with his address!

Smith peeled his car off of the back road he was on and headed for his house.

Once again, Detective Smith realized just how much time he spent out in the field instead of inside his own home. It was always this way with cases that had a small window of opportunity to catch the culprit. He shook away this thought and went into his living room where his directory was. Smith kept the directory inside one of his many desk drawers so that it was easy to get at if needed. He opened up the far left one and took out the little book. Flipping to the *T*s, the detective quickly located his mark.

Smith had his hand on the doorknob when he stopped and looked around his cozy house.

Funny how I chose my office to be in my house so that it would be easier to go between work and pleasure, yet I rarely have the time to enjoy it, Smith thought to himself. He vowed to make a change as he closed the front door of his house with one hand and held the newly written address in the other.

The monsoon had picked up to such an extent that it obscured the small building in front of Detective

Smith. From what he could perceive, it was just a modern home in a modern neighborhood. He went up to the wooden front door and knocked hard so that it was heard above the thunder and rain. To his surprise, a woman appeared on the threshold.

"Hello. What can I do for you?" the woman yelled.

"May I come in?" Smith yelled back. She motioned for him to do so while Smith said his thanks. The inside was about as modern as the outside. The whole picture told the story of the typical American family. "Is Dr. Wilson Thompson present?" he asked once the door had silenced the noise.

"I'm sorry, but Dr. Thompson moved out about three months ago," the woman said with an apologetic expression that matched her voice. She noticed the slip of paper in the detective's hand. "I was afraid this might happen. The old address hasn't been changed in the directory yet, if that is where you got it."

"No problem. Do you know where he is living currently?" Smith asked.

"Not to my knowledge. My husband might though. My name is Jenny, by the way. Devon!" she called out. A man appeared out of what seemed to be the kitchen and came to stand beside his wife. He looked just as good-natured as the person he married. "Do you by any chance know where the man who lived here before us is living now?"

A thoughtful expression came across the man's face. "Wilson Thompson? No, I don't remember where he said he was moving. It was all so hectic trying to get all of his things out and all of our stuff in," the man named Devon explained.

"Ah, I see."

"Sorry we couldn't be of any help, Mr.?"

"Detective Smith," Smith introduced, shaking both their hands.

"Detective Smith? We've heard a lot about you!" Jenny exclaimed.

"We keep up with a lot of your cases in the newspaper. The way you handled that kidnapping a couple months back was impressive," Devon added.

"Why, thank you very much. It's always nice to be appreciated. But usually, the police department partners on some cases that come my way. I would not have been able to solve a good many without their help," Smith said.

"Why don't you come and sit down?" Jenny asked, clearly excited that a well-known detective was in her house.

"I wouldn't want to intrude…"

"It's no bother!" the husband said.

"If you insist." Smith followed the happy couple into the main area of their house. It was stocked with comfortable looking furniture and a nice coffee table.

"May I get you something to drink?" Jenny asked.

"No, thank you," Smith whispered as Devon struck up a conversation.

"So you working on a big case?" he asked.

"All of my cases are pretty important, but this one is more so, yes."

"How so?" the wife had entered into the conversation with two hot drinks. She handed one to her husband, then sat down on the chair opposite the detective.

"We have reason to believe that Dr. Thompson has stolen a large sum of money from a client of mine and that he used some kind of modified injection system to do it," Detective Smith explained.

"Wow. He seemed very nice when we talked to him," Devon said.

"What did he say?" Smith asked, his attention perking up.

"Nothing much. Just said how crazy moving was. We felt sorry for him too. He had a lot of stuff to haul out."

"Did any of that stuff involve equipment that looked like it would fit in a hospital?" Devon looked at his wife who was concentrating on the question.

"More like the kind of things you would find in a science lab," Devon answered.

"A science lab?" Smith was immensely interested now.

"Mm-hmm. Strange beakers and test tubes. Also he had this box with a tarp over it. Whatever was inside of it must have been very important," Jenny said.

"And when we asked him about it, he gave a hurried answer. Something about experimenting with different kinds of medicine?" Devon threw in.

"I am very glad that you two noticed these things. They may come in handy in the investigation," Smith said.

"It was our pleasure, Detective! Oh, I just remembered one more thing. Right before Dr. Thompson left, he said something about how it would be much easier to get supplies. I'm not sure if he meant medical supplies or what," Jenny added.

"You guys have certainly shed some light on a few dark spots. If you need anything at all, don't hesitate to call," Smith said as he gave Devon his number.

"Will do, Detective! Thanks for dropping by!" Devon commented.

Smith glanced at a photograph lying on a table against the far wall. It showed Jenny pointing to a ring on her finger with a lake in the background. As he passed Devon, he whispered, "Get her something nice for her anniversary."

Before he could open the door, Devon came up to him. "Wait, how did you know our anniversary is soon?" Devon asked, clearly bewildered.

"The picture on the far table tells all you need to figure out that it is coming up. The fact that you just got married is evident by the fact that your wife is pointing to the ring. The rest is made clear in the background. That certain lake only opens its waters when summer comes around. The boat on the lake is relatively new, so it must have been bought before. I would say sometime in the winter. Also, the boat is a herring fishing boat. Herring only come out at the beginning of summer," Detective Smith concluded.

"Un-unbelievable..." Devon stammered.

"If you take what clues are around you, a bigger picture can emerge," Smith said, using the same concept that he had used earlier that day. He shook Devin's hand once more and left the happy couple to continue with their lives.

Once in his car, Smith realized the objective still remained the same: find the house of Wilson Thompson and investigate whether or not he was experimenting with ways to make injections less painful. Now armed with the new leads that had been given to him by the couple, he had pretty strong evidence against him. But in all his time as a detective, he had learned to never make an assumption based on data that cannot be backed up. He had learned to get all the information he could before making a theory. Never make facts suit theories. Instead, make theories so that they suit facts. This is why Detective Smith found himself tracking the home of a possible million-dollar-theft suspect.

A CLOSE CALL

Detective Smith walked out of his fourth supply store with no more information about where his suspect lived than when he started. He had tried asking around hardware stores, supermarkets, and local stores that sold medical supplies but to no avail. His trail on his suspect was starting to go cold, and the timeline was shortening. Smith got into his car and started his engine. The downpour was still falling hard around the detective. It was as if there had never been a time when it was not raining.

What do I know? I know the name and occupation of the culprit without a doubt. The only evidence I have as to where he lives is that he lives near a supply store. After checking half of the supply stores in town, that clue is starting to look not as effective as I originally thought. There has to be something that I am missing. I need to broaden my vision.

In his mind's eye, Smith went through all the streets and back roads that connected the city together. He ignored all the locations he had been in the past hour and concentrated on the part of town that he had not yet been to. Turning a corner on to a familiar street, a memory forced its way into Smith's vision. He remembered two years ago a case that had involved a locally known store. Smith took the case to train his new assistant, Riley, that had been assigned to him. There was a break-in, and physically, there was no evidence to convict the criminal. Detective Smith and his new right-hand man had successfully apprehended the culprit and put him behind bars. But what is more important than the outcome of the case—the name of the store. It was Carlton's Supply Emporium.

Smith pulled his mind back to the present in an instant. It wasn't *a* supply shop; it was *the* supply shop. When Wilson Thompson had said that he was going to be closer to a supply shop, he was hinting the actual name of the building. With the trail hot again, the detective sped off to ascertain the location of his prime suspect. His hunch may not pan out in the end, but at least Smith would be able to gain the location of the other stores should he require. Pulling into Carlton's Supply Emporium, Smith realized how out of the way this shop really was. Besides him, the parking lot was completely empty. He got out of his car and jogged to the two sliding doors that made the entrance to the small convenience store. The interior was empty except for the checkout workers. The moment he got into sight, the workers started yelling out deals and discounts that could be found on different aisles. Smith walked up to the nearest worker.

"Hello, good sir. How may I help you?" the worker asked with a theatrical tone.

"Do you know if a man by the name of Wilson Thompson shops here?" the detective responded.

"I don't know about that, but I have seen a man come here frequently for the past several weeks. Why do you need to know?"

"My name is Detective Smith, and I am investigating an ongoing case. Dr. Thompson may know something about the circumstances which surround it."

"No kidding, huh? Well, I'm not sure if that was him. I'm not really known for my memory," the worker revealed. The other worker adjacent to the one whom Smith was questioning caught some of the bits of conversation and walked over.

"I couldn't help overhear, but did you say that you need information on our newest regular? I just so happen to have a credit card receipt from the last time he was here," she said as she motioned Smith over to her checkout counter. She pulled up a list of clients on the monitor. "I can't believe that Dr. Thompson may be involved in a crime. He seemed like such a nice guy."

"We are not certain at this time if he is directly involved with what happened or not," Detective Smith said.

"I hope he's not. Anyway, is this what you are looking for?" While she was talking, the worker scanned through recent transactions and receipts until she stopped on one signed by a Wilson Thompson.

"Yes, thank you. Is there anyway that you can print it off?" Smith asked. In answer to his question, she clicked a few buttons that were accompanied shortly by a sound from the small receipt printer.

"Here you go," she said as she handed him the small slip of paper. Smith turned to leave when another question came to his mind.

"What exactly did Dr. Thompson buy?"

"Different kinds of medicine, some food, just your normal everyday stuff. Earlier this week, he bought some disinfectant spray and gauze. He was a doctor, so he probably just ran out of some supplies for his work."

"Thank you. You have been a great help," the detective said, leaving the woman to continue her work. Smith exited the small supply store with a couple more clues at his disposal.

Now we know for certain that Dr. Thompson has been shopping here the past few weeks. For him to even mention that he was moving closer to a supply shop, he would had to have been very close. I would wager inside a five-mile perimeter. That still doesn't tell as much about his location. Wait...No car was ever found around the abandoned shed where the crime took place. He was walking when he had to take cover behind the Dumpster. That means that he is close enough to walk to where he committed the crime but also close enough to where he can get in and out of a supply store quickly!

After finishing this thought process, Detective Smith decided to partake in an experiment. He held up his right hand and converted his watch from telling time to a stopwatch. Just as he hit Start, he pressed his foot on the accelerator. Taking the fastest way possible and brushing up against the limits of the speed for that road, he timed himself to find out how long it took to get from the supply store to the abandoned shed. There was no traffic on the back roads that Smith was taking, so stopping and starting wasted no time. He hit the Stop button just as he pulled up to the broken-down building. It took Smith nine minutes and thirty-seven seconds to get from one location to the other. Taking in to account that on any other day there would be some traffic, Smith figured it most likely took a maximum of ten minutes.

If Dr. Thompson wanted to get to both places with ease, then one would suspect that he would be right in the middle of both locations. But walking five miles would take time, even if you kept a steady jog. He would need to be closer to the shed rather than closer to the supply store.

Smith closed the door to his car before walking into the building where the crime was committed. The inside looked exactly the same as when he was here earlier that day. All the furniture was still scattered around the room, and if anything, the steps leading to the upper levels had deteriorated even more. Detective Smith took a good look around the main room, recalling everything that was said during his short visit. He walked over to the small table where the briefcase was sitting while the transaction was commencing. Examining the table in a minute way, he noticed that the legs of the table had sustained structural damage. The cracks on the wood looked fresher than the marks on the other wood in the house. Smith noticed that the whole table had a brighter tint in the wood than the rest of the house. He looked closer and realized that the whole table was relatively new. It wasn't as old as the house it was inside of.

Why would there be a new wooden table in an old, decaying house? It had to have been put there by someone. It was already there when I arrived, so no one on the police force could have put it there. Either Dr. Thompson or Mr.

Verner put it there. Since Mr. Verner was unconscious, he probably tried to protect the money himself. If he put the table there, he could set the briefcase on it and control how and when the money changed hands. But what he did not expect was opposition in his plan. So he sets the briefcase down on the table that he placed there beforehand, tries to take the money forcibly by taking out his gun, somehow manages to lose control of it, and the bullet causes everything to go black. Then Mr. Verner wakes up with no cognitive memory of what happened or how he got there. Smith stood up and gave a last look to the small table until moving on.

Once outside, Detective Smith jogged over to the only landmark that he knew about his suspect's midnight walk: the Dumpster. Tracing back the perpetrator's steps, Smith played the events of that night in reverse. Starting from the Dumpster, he walked in the opposite direction of the abandoned shed. The detective continued his trek until he came to the end of the street. Not many houses lined both sides of the street. This part of town was rarely visited and known by few. A perfect place to conduct a perfect crime. Overhead, lightning crackled and shot across the sky. It lit up the surrounding area for a split-second. While the world was bright, Smith saw a small street sign on the far side of the opposite street. He looked up and down the street, and then made a break for it. The sign indicated two ways: one that followed a paved road, which went deeper into the city, and one that went down a small dirt path, which went away from the city. Smith stopped and thought about his choices for a moment. Making his decision, he took the small dirt path. Smith broke into a jog after a few minutes of walking. Nothing along the path revealed anything to where the culprit lived. He was starting to get discouraged until he came to a small gate that indicated the end to the path. Another road branched off to the right of the metal gate. Detective Smith guessed that it would lead directly to the supply store he had just came from. Marking the location in his memory, Smith turned around and made his way back to his car. He was going to report to the chief about his finding.

The buzz of excitement hit Detective Smith as he entered into the police headquarters. He spotted a couple familiar faces that proceeded to give him a wave and a thumbs-up. Smith walked up to the receptionist, who gave him the same smile that he was seeing on many of the officers.

"Hello, Detective! Perfect timing!" she said with enthusiasm.

"Judging by the atmosphere, I would say that something big is going on. Did you guys solve a cold case?" Smith asked.

"You never cease to impress me, Detective. Not only did we solve a cold case, but also the way we solved it was by solving another case. You may remember the chief talking about a certain case he was working on? It turns out that the person who committed that crime also committed another crime that has been cold for over ten years," she explained.

"Very impressive! Speaking of the chief, do you know where I can find him? I have some new information regarding the investigation."

"Today just keeps getting better and better! He should be in his office."

"Thank you. Good luck out here!" Smith called.

On his way into the chief's office, he ran into two reporters who looked like they had just gotten their news for tonight. Inside, he found the chief and Jefferson in conversation with each other.

"You were right, Jefferson, when you said that reporters have a sixth sense for this kind of thing."

"It's almost like they can smell anything connected to crime from one hundred miles away. I'm not sure if—Detective! Nice to see you again!" Jefferson said, noticing the new addition to the office.

"Likewise," Smith answered, shaking the young deputy's hand.

"So, Detective, have you made any more progress on your case?" the chief asked.

"Yes, Chief, I have. I know that Wilson Thompson moved to a house that is both within close proximity to the abandoned shed of this morning and a locally known supply store."

"How did you figure that out?" Jefferson asked, once again anxious to hear of the detective's ways.

"Once I knew the culprit's name, things became both easier and harder. I looked up his name in my address book only to find that the house listed there now belongs to a very nice couple. While I was there, they told me that Dr. Thompson had equipment that looked like it would be at home in a science lab. They also told me that he carried out a device that had a sheet over it. When the couple asked him about it, he gave a hurried answer about experimenting with different kinds of medicines. Jenny, the wife, remembered hearing him say that it would be easier to go to the supply store once he moved. I tracked down the supply store and got confirmation that he indeed did shop there. From there, I calculated his whereabouts and best to my knowledge, have found where he lives," Smith explained.

"I don't see how you do it, Detective," the chief said.

"Amazing," Jefferson remarked, once again highly impressed by the detective's work methods

"But enough about me, what happened here? I heard that you solved two cases? One a cold case, no doubt."

"It was mostly Jefferson here," the chief said.

"Please, Chief. You're the one who found him and cornered him," Jefferson responded.

"Yes, but you are the one who shot the gun out of his hand then drop tackled him."

"Not many deputies can say that they have done that. Nice job," Smith said.

"It was nothing, Detective. Just doing my job," Jefferson said, clearly uplifted by the detective's words.

"Have you had the time to search Thompson's house yet, Detective?"

"Actually, Chief, that's why I'm here. Is there anyway that you can get a warrant to search it?"

"No problem, Detective. Knowing you, you probably have enough evidence to get one," the chief said with a smile.

"I believe I do," Smith concurred.

"Then let's catch ourselves a thief. Jefferson? Can you go get a warrant for the detective here?"

"Yes, sir. Right away." Jefferson bounded off to his next assignment, driven to do better by Smith's success. Ten minutes later, the chief, Jefferson, Detective Smith, and a squad of policemen raced off to the location that Smith had indicated with a warrant in hand.

"Blasted rain… Gets everything muddy," the chief said as he led the way down the small dirt path. When they came to the gate, the procession found that it was swinging wide open in the wind.

"That's peculiar. It was locked when I came here last," Smith said in a questioning tone.

"The wind must have blown it open," Jefferson responded. The chief pulled his car as close to the front door as he could without knocking it down. All three of them got out of his car and made their way to the front entrance. The chief pounded on the wooden door.

"Open up! We have a warrant to search your house!"

When no one answered, the chief signaled for his men to cover him. He backed up a few feet and kicked the handle of the door with such force that it blew out the lock. The chief did a quick sweep of the entrance hall and told his men to check the rest of the house. Detective Smith heard many "Clears!" as he made his way through the front hall. It was a moderately sized house with stairs leading to an upper level. The living room was stocked with only a small couch and a long table. The suspect's house looked like any average home; nothing suspicious met their eyes.

"Chief, Detective. You might want to see this," Jefferson called from the kitchen. The kitchen matched the rest of the house in terms of normality. It had everything that your typical kitchen has: a stove, a microwave, a sink, a pantry, and an oven.

"Thompson's house is about as normal as you can get," the chief remarked.

"I'm not so sure," Jefferson said as he opened the refrigerator.

"Looks like we found the right place," the chief said. There was only one thing in the refrigerators: syringes. Detective Smith wrapped his hand around one of the many cold cylinders that lined the racks.

"Prototypes," he said after inspecting them. No syringe was the same. They ranged from the basic long tube like structure with a singular needle, to short rectangles with two short needles protruding out.

"He must have been here awhile to have time to make all of these," Jefferson said, picking one of the prototypes up and scrutinizing one for himself.

"From what I have investigated, he has been here only a few months," Smith responded.

"Only several months to make all of those? Thompson is one heck of a doctor. Or scientist. Whichever," the chief said.

"The only problem is which one did he settle on?" Smith said, as if asking the very objects themselves.

"My question is, where is his work station?" Jefferson asked. Smith thought about the layout of the house he was standing in.

"It must be in the upper level. That way if anyone came by, they would not see it," Smith said.

"Let's go find out for ourselves," the chief said, leading the way through the living room and up the stairs. While Smith was following the chief to the upper level, he noticed small, dark spots that were seared into the carpet. Once the trio was up the stairs, one of the officers clicked on the light, illuminating a strange object in the center of the room.

"What in the world is that?" Jefferson asked, slowly walking toward the machine. The center of the object had a massive chamber, which branched off into tubes that led to a smaller chamber on the top. In between both chambers was a miniature-sized area contained by two steel plates. On the bottom plate, it had ten holes that matched the ten holes on the exact opposite side. The whole machine totaled to about three feet tall.

"I have no idea, but whatever it is, it's still hot," the chief said in answer to Jefferson's questions. Detective Smith went over to the strange object and passed his hand over it.

"The chief's correct. Some type of heat source has been used here recently," Smith said. He leaned in closer to the machine. "I would say that those holes on the bottom plate are on an ignition system. The flames came out of the holes to slowly melt whatever is lying in between."

"Why are there two sets of holes if just one is needed?" the chief asked.

"My guess would be that the second set of holes are there to allow whatever the after product is of the melting to pass through," Smith explained.

"Like a liquid to a gas," Jefferson said.

"Exactly." The chief slowly started walking around the machine, inspecting every angle of the strange find. He came to the side opposite Smith and Jefferson and came to a halt.

"He sure had a view," the chief commented about the window he was now standing in front of.

"He sure did. You can see everything from out here. There's the gate that we came in from and there are our cars," Jefferson said, coming over to see for himself. Detective Smith eyed the window and its convenient proximity to the machine.

"Dr. Thompson saw us coming," Smith said, more to himself than to the others.

"Even if he did see us coming, there is no way that he would have known at what time," the chief said. Detective Smith walked over to the window.

"He could see everything. From the minute that we were at his gate, he had eyes on us. Most likely, he spotted me when I came here beforehand."

"But how would he escape?" the chief asked, this being the first time he did not hit his mark. He was trying very hard to protect his reputation as the utmost force at the station.

"He must have left right when he saw us because he didn't have time to grab that," Jefferson said, nodding toward the machine.

"Officer Trueman's hypothesis is spot on," Smith said.

"What's our next move, Detective?" the chief asked.

"I think that we have exhausted all the evidence we can out of this house, I suggest—" Smith spotted something on the carpet that put an end to what he was going to say. He kneeled down to observe the mark in the carpet that matched the abrasions on the stairs. He stood, his mind working fast. He walked from his position from the window to the machine. Observing similar marks there also, he smiled one of his rare, triumphant smiles. Piecing together what he found downstairs with what he observed upstairs, he came to a conclusion.

"What is it, Detective?" Jefferson asked enthusiastically.

"I know what this machine is. It is called a chemical converter."

"A chemical converter? I remember running into one of those during a drug bust. Some whack job was trying to combine different types of drugs together. Except, I don't remember it being as big and as complicated as this one," the chief said.

"That is because this one was being used to combine different types of chemicals and medicines," Smith said, remembering the grocery list that would normally be commonplace.

"What was he using a chemical converter for?" Jefferson asked.

"I have no theories yet, but in time, it will become clear."

"Well, I vote that we get out of here. Besides, it's dinner time soon, and I'm thinking Italian," the chief said, his hunger getting the better of him.

"I couldn't agree more, Chief," Smith said.

"Hey, why don't you join us?" Jefferson asked.

"I wouldn't want to intrude," Smith started.

"You wouldn't be intruding, Detective. And besides, the more the merrier," the chief said.

"If you insist."

On the way back down, the chief dismissed all the officers that he brought along. Once again, it was just the detective, Jefferson, and the chief. When they left the house, they found that the torrential rain was still falling hard. The chief threw a sigh to the clouds, hoping that it would be enough to plug them. They all found their way to the chief's car dripping wet. While Jefferson and the chief conversed about the annoyance of the constant rain, Smith's phone buzzed quietly in his coat pocket.

"Hello, this is Detective Smith… Mr. Savage, how do you do? Yes. Yes… We have made progress on your case. As of right now, we have narrowed it down to one suspect… That's the problem. He is not as easy to apprehend as I originally thought… Don't worry we will get your money back safe and sound… You had a Where's Benjamin? One of those dollar bills that you can track to see where it goes? It was a hundred-dollar bill that you could track? I thought that they only made bills like that from ones to twenties. Uh-huh. They only made five? What is the importance of them? Oh, so only five are out there each bearing a name of a different state that was stamped on it and you had the one from this state? Okay, I understand… Do not worry, Mr. Savage, we will get your money back. Your Where's Benjamin and all." Once Smith hung up his phone, his other two companions concluded their conversation about the rain.

"He has a Where's Benjamin?" Jefferson asked, wide-eyed.

"Yes. It was part of his money that got stolen. I didn't even know that they existed," Smith replied.

"You learn something new every day," the chief said.

"Indeed, you do," Smith concurred.

"I used to collect Where's Georges when I was younger… Good times," Jefferson said, his mind in the past. "It was always my dream to get a Where's Benjamin…"

"Anyway, Detective, what did Savage want?"

"He was wondering how the case was coming along."

"What did you tell him?"

"I told him that we had narrowed it down to one suspect, but he evaded us."

"We'll get him eventually. He can't run for long," the chief said with vigor in his voice. They sat in silence for a few moments, each thinking about the case and the prey that had eluded them. The chief brought his car into the parking lot of the well-known Italian restaurant Lieto Tempos. The parking lot was packed full of cars, granted that it was a Friday night. The trio got out of the chief's car and made their way into the restaurant. The aroma of gourmet Italian food hit them like a wave as they entered.

"So, Detective, what was your hardest case in your career as a fighter of crime?" Jefferson asked, kicking off the conversation. Smith thought for a moment about all the cases that had ever come his way.

"Without a doubt, the spree of crimes that was committed about four years ago. The chief most likely remembers the events that followed the robbery of the electronics store," Smith started to explain.

"An electronics store? Sounds like your run-of-the-mill crime to me," Jefferson said.

"It did to me also, except for the fact that there was absolutely no evidence to be found anywhere on the crime scene to incriminate a suspect. When we got there, all the entrances were locked, windows sealed, and air ducts closed. There was no access point from which the culprit got in. All the items on the shelves were gone. If you walked into that store, it would appear to be an empty building," Smith concluded.

"Wow. Did you catch whoever did it?"

"Yes, but at a cost," the chief answered. The waiter interrupted Jefferson from further questions by bringing their meal. Their conversations drifted into different avenues until it settled upon family life.

"So, Chief, how is the family?" Jefferson asked.

"They're doing good. The wife is a little upset since I have been absorbed by our recent case, but what can you do? Crime doesn't wait for you to be ready. What about you, Jefferson? You hope to settle down one day?" the chief said with a shrug.

"Eventually, yes. But as of right now, I'm happy with where I am."

"That's good. How about you, Detective? How did you get into the crime business?" the chief asked, switching the spotlight to Smith.

"When I was younger, I saw whole families destroyed by crime. Innocent men and woman wrongfully convicted because evidence was looked at in a wrong way or completely missed altogether. I have dedicated my life to fighting such things, and when I see the culprit put behind bars to answer for his actions, it is all worth it. But deep down inside, I believe that good still lies in even the most hardened of hearts," Smith concluded, reminiscing on the past.

The conversation veered away from occupations until the waiter brought the check. Once it was paid, the trio got up to leave the restaurant. After thanking the waitress, the chief, the detective, and Jefferson closed the door to the delectable restaurant and made their way to the chief's car. Jefferson ran ahead with the keys in hand to pull the car around to save time. Smith was pondering their next move when a small object caught his attention through the mist. He left the chief, who was trying to open his umbrella to no avail, at the door and slowly fought his way through the flooded parking lot to the singular piece of paper lying on the ground. All his thoughts were shattered as he bent and picked up the rectangular-shaped item. The headlights of the car illuminated the object in his hand. A white one-hundred-dollar bill met Smith's eyes followed by a red circle stamped directly in the center of the bill.

It read, "Where's Benjamin? Go online and track your bill!" The name of one state was printed on the right hand side.

"He was here the whole time…"

EXTREME MEASURES

Detective Smith had entered back into the restaurant to interview possible witnesses and find out if anybody strange had come in before or while they were seated. He passed the chief who was on the phone with the police HQ ordering a perimeter seal off. On the chief's orders, Jefferson had taken his car to try and track down the suspect if he was on foot. Smith got a few questioning glances as he walked back into the restaurant.

"Hello, my name is Detective Smith," he said to the waitress. A look of recognition passed over her.

"Hey, I know you! I've read about you in the paper! What can I do for you?" she said excitedly.

"Has anyone strange come in tonight?"

"Why? Are you tracking somebody?" she asked enthusiastically.

"We have reason to believe that a Dr. Wilson Thompson is responsible for a crime and that he ate here tonight," Smith explained quickly.

"A criminal ate at my restaurant? No way!"

"Have you seen anyone different tonight?" Smith pushed, time being of the essence.

"Hmm. Oh! There was this one guy. He was in a business suit and had a very stylish fedora that covered most of his face. He also had on a single black glove on his left hand. It looked to me that he was trying to rip off Michael Jackson, except that his was white, not black… But still! And when he paid, he paid with cash, and I noticed that he was loaded!" the waitress said.

"Thank you. You have been a great help," Smith replied, exiting the store. Outside, everything seemed quiet and empty. The only other person in the parking lot was the chief, who had just finished his conversation with the station.

"Was it our guy?" he asked, coming over to the detective.

"It was. The waitress said that he paid with cash and had much of it. She also said he was dressed in a business suit, had a fedora, and a singular black glove on his left hand," Smith explained.

"A black glove?"

"If her account is accurate, then yes."

"But what for?" the chief asked, very confused.

"I am in the dark as of right now. Is Deputy Trueman still out in the field?"

"I was just about to call him and tell him to stop searching. It's nearly impossible to find anything in this weather," the chief said, once again shooting an angry look at the sky. Smith nodded his agreement. "How did he know that we were going to be here?"

"I am almost positive that he did not know he was going to be in the same room as the three people who want to catch him the most," Smith said.

"Why was he eating here then?" the chief asked, his mind still concentrated on the effort to seal off the surrounding areas. Detective Smith drew up the picture of the refrigerator that was barren except for the syringes in his mind.

"Dr. Thompson had an empty house, save for his equipment. With all the money he acquired, he has most likely been eating at restaurants since there was no food to be found anywhere in his house."

"That way, he could concentrate on his work and not have to cook!" the chief finished.

"My thoughts also," Smith agreed. The chief looked around at all the cars, wishing he were drying off in his.

"Other than that bill, we have no other hints as to where he is going or what he was doing."

"Then I suggest that we follow bread crumbs," the detective responded as he walked back to where he found the lead. He placed the bill in the position that he found it on the ground. He drew an imaginary line in his mind from the entrance of Lieto Tempos to the one-hundred-dollar bill. Continuing the line through the bill and out the other side, he followed it to the far side of the parking lot with the chief on his heels. Detective Smith came to a stop at one of the many parking places that made the outside edge. He knelt down and inspected the asphalt minutely. Two thick, black marks were visible with enough space in between to place a car. "Supposing that the culprit ran directly from the door to his destination, dropping the incriminating bill along the way, my hypothesis is that he parked here. Observe the two tire marks. Whoever was in that car wanted to get away in a hurry," Smith concluded.

"Amazing, Detective. If we had more people like you on the force, there would be nobody that we couldn't catch," the chief said.

"Do not discredit your team, Chief. There are many things that an official force can do that I cannot. For example, I cannot obtain warrants or call in assistance if need be. I also do not have the luxury of working as part of a unit, except for the occasional case where you lend a helping hand. We need both policemen and detectives alike to accomplish our goals."

"You are right, Detective, as always." Smith took another, closer look at the tire marks.

"If I only knew as much about cars as I do about crime. You wouldn't happen to know what kind of marks these are, would you, Chief?" Smith asked. The chief bent over to get a good look at the black streaks. A smile crossed over his face.

"I haven't seen one of these in years!"

"These tracks are familiar to you?"

"Absolutely. These are Plymouth Prowler tracks. Yup, small tires in front, big in back. I used to drive one back in the glory days," the chief said, picturing his old car in his mind.

"Well done, Chief!"

"Thank you, Detective. Let me get an all-points bulletin out. Shouldn't be that hard to find," the chief said, dialing up the police HQ's number. "It's the chief. Get an APB out on a Prowler… Our suspect drives one. Thanks." The chief canceled the call and turned to Smith. "It shouldn't take long to find him, but in this weather, you never really know."

"Then, I guess the only thing we can do for now is to wait," Smith said.

"Looks like it. Where is Jefferson with my car?" the chief sighed. As if on cue, Jefferson pulled into the parking lot, sliding on the wet asphalt and drifting into the parking spot closest to them.

"I did not mean to do that," Jefferson said as he threw open the passenger door. On the way to Smith's car, the detective and the chief filled in Jefferson with everything that they found. "Wow. So we really did just eat in the same restaurant with a criminal who got away in one of the coolest old cars ever. I'm glad you guys found something. I could not see anything in this storm, let alone find any trace of our man," Jefferson said as he pulled the car up to the abandoned shed where Smith had parked his car hours ago. "It sure does look creepy at night."

Detective Smith opened the door of the chief's car and got out. Instead of walking to his car, Smith entered into the condemned building for the third time that day. He stood in the center of the house, taking in every small detail.

All right, I know there has to be something that I am missing. The timetable just doesn't line up. Mr. Savage said that he discovered his safe was broken into early this morning. The crime happened late last night, and his safe was intact when he went to bed. That means that one of the culprits had to have time to break into his safe without him knowing, sneak the money out of the house, and come directly here. Unless he knew the code, whoever broke into it would have to use tools without a doubt. He would not have had the opportunity to hide them somewhere. He must have brought them here! But where would he place them…

Detective Smith went through the living room, crossing off all the places that he already knew a tool was not. He finished his inspection of the living room and moved into the kitchen. It seemed to be the only area in the house that was not fully affected by deterioration. The counters looked like they had seen some hard times but nevertheless had pushed on. One of the cabinet's hinges was broken, the rest being on the floor. A piece of the counter was nicked off, presumably when the cabinet door fell.

He most likely would hide them so that if the police did somehow get inside the house, they would not find them. That makes the cabinets not a viable hiding spot. There is no refrigerator or pantry, so that is out of the question.

Smith noticed a back door tucked away behind some debris that had fallen from the ceiling above. He rearranged the rubble so he could pass by without trouble. Smith turned the doorknob hard, only to find that it was locked. *What now?* He bent down to move a small piece of wood when he saw four small squares imprinted into the rotting wood that made up the floor. *Now what could that be?* He made his way back into the main kitchen area to look for whatever made the strange design on the floor. Smith noticed a chair that only had three legs leaning against the far wall.

Strange... The wood where the fourth leg was is cleanly broken. If it was worn down over time, it would not be so cut and dry. Unless someone wanted to make it look like it had just eroded and broke it off to prevent anyone from accessing something.

Smith grabbed the three-legged chair and aligned it with three of the four imprints. Seeing that a fourth was leg was needed, he took one of the smaller pieces of debris and propped it up as a makeshift leg. He stepped onto the chair, gingerly at first to test his weight. Finding that it would hold him, he stood up to his full height. In front of him, there was a little nook that was previously hidden by the ceiling. Smith felt a slight breeze from his right and turned to find a small grate that connected to a tunnel that led outside the house.

Looks like I have found my hiding place, he thought as he removed the grate. Inside the small alcove he found a chisel, a hammer, and an empty metal container. Smith took the tools out of their hiding place and left the abandoned shack once and for all.

Detective Smith's home was dark and quiet when he walked in. He went to his kitchen, put some coffee on, and made his way to his desk. When he sat down, he saw the now exhausted leads that he had written up earlier in the case. He looked at them long and hard, then sat them to the far side of his desk. Smith opened one of his many drawers to reveal documents and records of his cases and their outcomes. He noticed the file from his most difficult and dangerous case protruding out of the middle of the stack. The memories of that case came flooding back to his mind. With an effort, he pulled his mind to what he was doing in the present. He grabbed a pen and an envelope from behind the case reports. He took up his pen and started to write a letter. The ding of his coffee machine signaled that his drink was done. The sound of the rain picked up as he returned to the desk with his freshly brewed coffee. Minutes passed by in silence.

A noise outside made Detective Smith look up. He strained to hear over the continuous noise of the rain. It had been a barely audible sound, just enough of a disruption to grab Smith's attention. He heard it again, this time louder. Smith put his pen down and listened intently. A scraping metal on metal sound came from behind his front door. The detective turned off his small desk lamp right as the lock broke. He heard his door slowly creak open through the darkness. Smith could not see a foot in front of him, but he knew the layout of the house, and whoever had just busted the lock was standing ten yards in front of him. Smith crept noiselessly through to the half wall that separated the entry hall from the office. Peering ever so carefully around his hiding spot, Smith could see the intruder silhouetted against the stormy background. He carried a handgun in his hand and a long knife at his belt. He took a few cautious steps forward while Detective Smith got into position behind the small wall.

The intruder raised his hand that held the gun and continued to walk down the entryway. He looked into the detective's office, not expecting what was about to happen. While his face was turned toward Smith's direction, Smith bounded from his hiding spot throwing an open-palmed punch to the man's nose. His action took the man completely by surprise and caused him to reel back in pain. During this period of surprise,

Smith seized the hand that the gun was in and emptied the cartridge into the floor. His assailant swung widely in the direction that he thought the detective was in. Smith easily dodged it, slipped around him, and countered by hitting a pressure point on his leg. While he was on the ground, Smith turned on the lights to get a better look at the attacker. He had a rough look to him that matched perfectly to the scar that spanned one side of his face to the other.

"Who hired you?" Smith asked the man in a calm voice. He gave a menacing smile while taking out the knife from his belt in response. He charged Smith with more energy than he would have given his attacker credit for. He stabbed forward while going up with the knife. Smith underestimated the ferocity of the strike, sidestepping just in time. Still, the sharp blade scored a gash in the detective's left arm. Blocking out the pain, Smith prepared for the next set of attacks. This time, the man swung with his left arm. Smith saw the feint that was coming by the tense in muscles on the knife hand. He ducked inside the punch, making it almost impossible for the man to slash with his knife. But his arm was already in motion. When the strike was at its apex, Smith grabbed the man's wrist, dislocating it. His calculated strike caused the man to drop his weapon and fall to his knees in pain. The detective picked up the knife and laid it on his desk. Smith took out his cell phone and called the chief. "Chief, it's Detective Smith. I have got someone here that you might be interested in."

Moments later, Detective Smith's assailant was being loaded into the back of a police car. The chief and his deputy had answered the call right away, getting there mere minutes after the call was made.

"You all right, Detective?" the chief asked, walking up to him and pointing at his wound.

"Yes, one of your very qualified medics saw to it," Smith answered.

"Good. How exactly did he sneak up on you?"

"He used the cover of the storm to mask his intentions. I was barely able to make out him breaking my lock."

"But it still wasn't enough," Jefferson said, joining in with the conversation.

"I am fortunate that he didn't have experience with this kind of thing. And little did my attacker know that I have studied, and become quite proficient in, the eclectic martial art known as Bartitsu. All in all, I could be in a lot worse shape than I am right now," Smith said.

"Where did he come from?" the chief asked.

"He recently got released from prison. Been in there for five years until last week. At least now, he will have a story to tell his buddies in there," Jefferson said. He had looked into the man's file once he was in custody.

"It seems awfully convenient how the same night that we get the closest to catching Thompson is the same night that a hit man comes to your house, Detective," the chief said.

"We do not know for sure if the two are connected yet, Chief," Smith said.

"In my eyes, they are." After Smith's attacker was taken to the police station, the chief and Jefferson soon followed him out. Detective Smith walked back inside his house to try and get some sleep for the following day.

The mornings resembled the nights when constant rain was present. While Smith was eating his breakfast, the chief called. "Good morning, Chief! You found the suspect's car? All right, I will be right over." The second day of investigation had already begun. He jotted down the address of the location of the car and headed out the door, leaving an unfinished meal in his wake.

"A policeman found it out here while on patrol," the chief said when Smith pulled up.

"Any damage to it?" Smith asked.

"None that we can see, but we don't have a trained eye at detail like yours." The Prowler was abandoned on the side of the road in what appeared to be the middle of nowhere. Detective Smith and the chief walked to the forensics expert who was examining it.

"Hello again, Detective Smith. Figured I would see you here," Bernard from the Forensics Department said.

Smith shook his hand. "Likewise. What do we got?"

"Nothing much, really. The ignition shows signs of scratching, but that's probably from the key. I have some of my guys dusting for prints."

"So Dr. Thompson drives out to the middle of nowhere, then just drops his car off and walks back? Somebody else had to be involved," Smith said. Bernard pointed at Smith then got back to work inspecting the car.

"Verner might have helped Thompson out by picking him up," the chief suggested.

"Possibly, but Mr. Verner does not remember anything involving the crime. He might not even remember Dr. Thompson," Smith said.

"Good point. But all Thompson had to do was bribe him with money and tell him to pick him up. Verner wouldn't have to know one thing,"

"True."

"That's about all we can do, Chief. Once we run those fingerprints, we will know who has been here," Bernard said, walking over to the two. He took off his glasses and cleared the lens.

"Thanks, Bernard. If you find anything else out, give me a shout."

"Will do, Chief. Come on, boys, we're pulling out!" Bernard and his fellow forensics workers left the rundown Prowler and went back to the HQ.

"Well, Detective, now that this has become attempted murder, I'll need to settle some things at the station. I forgot to mention on the phone that the guy who attacked you talked. Said a large man with a Scottish accent hired him. It puts a whole new spin on things so I better get to work. Good luck, Detective!" the chief called as he got into his car and drove away.

Once he was alone, Smith inspected the abandoned car for himself. It appeared to be your classic drop-the-car-and-run scheme. Like the forensics expert had said, nothing out of the ordinary struck the detective's well-trained eye. The ignition was indeed scuffed up from something metal. Everything that he saw collaborated what Bernard had said.

Nothing seems to be out of the ordinary, Smith thought as he inspected the whole driver's side of the car. His eyes drifted to the passenger side where he noticed something out of place. Muddy footprints were imprinted upon the floor of the passenger side.

Why would there be footprints on only one side of the car? Where I am standing there is no mud, but the other side is covered in it. If Dr. Thompson was in a hurry, then why wouldn't he abandon the car and run?

Smith carefully avoided the mud as he made his way over to the passenger side to inspect it.

These prints are not from the forensics experts because they were wearing the crime scene shoes so as not to contaminate evidence. They were left by Dr. Thompson, but why? One footprint is facing the glove compartment, I wonder…

Detective Smith reached over and popped the opening on the glove compartment. The inside of the alcove contrasted the car to the letter. It was dented and scratched as if someone had tried to shove something in that did not fit.

Whatever was in here is what Dr. Thompson was after. The dimensions of the glove compartment could fit a small rectangle object, but what about a large rectangle object?

In his mind, Smith extended the space out to compensate for all the dents. Matching up all the major scratches, Smith drew an imaginary line between them. Taking the larger cracks as corners, he filled in all the space he had drawn with his lines and got his shape.

The briefcase was never found at the crime scene. With Mr. Verner unconscious, the only person who could have taken it is Dr. Thompson. He most likely thrust it into the glove compartment with force, causing the dents and abrasions. Then, when he abandoned the car, he snatched the briefcase and went on his way. But why is that briefcase so important? I think it is high time we find out.

Detective Smith stopped by his house on the way to his next lead to grab a few items. After entering his house, he made his way to the kitchen. He saw the tools that were used for the breaking of the safe lying on his counter. Picking them up, he headed back out into the still pounding rain. It had died down ever so slightly since last night's excursions. Smith looked around his house hoping that the culprit would be put behind bars soon. He spied the half-written letter on his desk, interrupted from its goal by the attacker. Walking over to his desk, he took the letter into his hands and read what had been written so far. Smith almost took out his pen and finished the letter had it not been for the time frame that was coming to a close every so quickly before him. He replaced the letter on his desk, gave it a quick glance, and got back in his car.

TYING UP LOOSE ENDS

Detective Smith dialed the number of his next target while recalling the address. "Mr. Savage? It's Detective Smith… The case is going well… We found the suspect's car. He cannot be far from us now… No, nothing of evidence could be found. But that is the reason that I called. One of the reason's actually. Have you moved your safe since it was broken into? You haven't? Very good! I very possibly might have found the tools that did the deed. I was inquiring if I could test my hypothesis… Great! I will see you there." Smith hung up his line, preparing for the first time in his life to break into a safe.

Mr. Savage's house concealed the wealth that he had. It was a small, single-storied house, with the backside facing parts of a forest. The front door opened directly into the living room with the kitchen attached. Mr. Savage answered the door after half of the first ring of the doorbell. His appearance was the same as the day that Smith met him. He was still haggard looking and wore an expression of never-ending tiredness. "Come in, Detective. Man, am I glad to see you." Mr. Savage led Smith over to the safe that was adjacent to the far wall. "This is it. This is where my whole life savings was stolen from me," Savage said with despair.

"Do not fret, Mr. Savage. I have the utmost confidence that we will retrieve your money safe and sound," Smith reassured.

This seemed to take some of the uneasiness out of Savage's voice. "So you think that you know how they did it?"

"I believe so," Smith said with a nod. The safe in question was indeed broken into. The whole lock looked as if it had been shattered by a jackhammer. Oddly enough, the surrounding areas looked as good as new. "This is very peculiar."

"Why is that?"

"The whole area where the lock used to be is completely missing. See? For someone to get that effect, they would have to use very powerful tools," Smith said.

"Are you saying that someone snuck in here in the middle of the night and used industrial tools to break my safe," Savage exclaimed.

"I do not think so. If those types of tools were used, then the surrounding areas would have felt the effect. Not to mention that the loud noise would have woken you up."

"How did they do it then?" Savage asked, curious.

Detective Smith took up the hammer and chisel and aimed it at the spot where the lock resided.

"Using the technique of the hammer and chisel would not result in a full shattering effect. They had to have used something of a higher caliber."

"But what?"

"That is the question." They both sat in silence, contemplating the many ways a lock can be shattered.

Mr. Savage broke the silence. “You said on the phone that you had two things that you wanted to figure out. One was the lock, what was the other?”

“At the crime scene yesterday morning, we discovered everything that could give us a case. Except that one thing was missing: a briefcase. I followed up on that lead only for the trail to die off. I did not think it was of much importance until we found the culprit’s car.”

“You said that nothing was found in his car,” Savage asked, momentarily confused.

“It is occasionally what you do not find that makes all the difference. After closer inspection, I found that a very large rectangular-shaped object had been forced into the glove box.”

“The briefcase.”

“Precisely,” Smith said.

“What is so important about a briefcase that it must be carried around all the time?” Savage asked.

“That is my question as well. But there is something else that I want to ask. Did you notice a briefcase to go missing the same day that you realized your money was also gone?” Savage thought a moment before answering.

“Now that you mention it, yes! I thought that I had just misplaced it. That was my best one too!” Savage said.

“Was there anything particularly remarkable about the briefcase? “

“Not really. I bought it a few years back for business. It had a thin layer of lead so it would be more durable. But other than that, nothing too special,” Savage explained.

"Was your briefcase empty?" Smith questioned, fearing the worst.

Savage's face got even more haggard looking. "Why do things keep getting worse and worse? I had bought tickets for a vacation with Wilson Thompson that I have been planning for a couple months and he wanted me to hold on to them. The plane takes off today. I kept both tickets inside the briefcase, so I wouldn't lose them. A lot of good that did me," Savage said as he collapsed on a chair. The stress of having his money taken from him was taking its toll.

"Mr. Savage, you have my word that you will have your money back in less than a day. We are closing in on him. He has nowhere to run now. Which airport are those tickets for?"

"The downtown airport," Savage said sadly.

"If I find any new evidence, I will contact you," Smith said as he dialed the chief's number and left Mr. Savage's home. "Chief, if you are not in the process of doing something, make your way to the downtown airport… The briefcase that was stolen had tickets for a plane that takes off today. I am on my way there right now… All right." Detective Smith sped toward the airport, hoping that he wasn't too late. He pulled into an empty parking space, jammed his car into park, and flew out of his door in a matter of seconds. Smith sprinted to the revolving doors and ran inside. He searched the baggage line for anyone that was wearing a black glove.

"Have you seen anybody today that has had a singular black glove on his left hand?" Smith asked the baggage checkout receptionist. She shook her head no with a very confused expression on her face. Smith turned again to scan the line when he heard the sound of sirens behind him. The chief's car and a black and white pulled up to the airport. Jefferson and his boss got out and ran inside.

"Any luck?" Jefferson asked, he too scanning the line.

"Unfortunately not. The receptionist said that she hasn't seen anyone with a black glove all day," Smith explained shortly.

"Do you think that he is already past security?" the chief asked.

"Most likely not. Everyone that comes through here had to go through baggage. A man with a black glove would stand out in a crowd."

"The receptionist said that the next flight doesn't take off for another couple hours," a lady officer said. Smith recognized her from the abandoned shed of yesterday morning.

"All right, thanks. Get a few more officers and stake out every car that comes here until that flight takes off. If anyone comes with a black glove or looks suspicious, flag him down," the chief ordered.

"Yes, sir," she said, snapping off a quick salute and leaving to fulfill her duties.

"Did Mr. Savage say anything else?" Jefferson asked.

"I inspected his safe that was broken into and found that whoever cracked it was very skillful. The whole lock was shattered, but the surrounding areas were not even scathed," Smith recounted.

Jefferson's eyes narrowed. "Let me guess, the tools that were used were a hammer and a chisel," he said suspiciously.

"Exactly. How did you know?"

"I cannot believe somebody actually did it successfully," Jefferson said, shaking his head.

"What do you mean, Jefferson?" the chief asked with a sigh.

"Before I came to work under you, Chief, there was a similar case with a broken safe that I worked. The safe looked exactly how the detective described. The lock was completely shattered, with no damage to any other part of the safe. The guy who did it used liquid nitrogen to freeze the lock and then hit it with the chisel while the hammer was against it to break the lock, causing it to shatter like ice. The only problem was that when he sprayed the lock, he forgot to move his hand. Froze three of his fingers in his right hand. The doctors had to amputate. Luckily, he was not very skilled and froze the surrounding areas, making it impossible to shatter the lock," Jefferson concluded.

"That would account for the strange metal container that I found along with the chisel and hammer," Smith said.

"That makes sense. He put the liquid nitrogen in the container, snuck over to Mr. Savage's house, and stole the money," Jefferson responded.

"Nice job, Jefferson," the chief said, giving him a pat on the back.

"Thanks, Chief."

"Well, Detective, what do we do now? Wait?" the chief inquired.

"That is the best course of action that I can see," Detective Smith answered.

"We'll give you a heads up if anything happens," the chief said. He motioned for Jefferson to follow then exited the airport. Smith could see that the officers were already in position once he was outside again. He made his way back to his car that was parked a little ways. He shut the car door and started up the engine. Smith closed his eyes and thought back to every detail that this case had given him. Starting from the minute that he stepped into the condemned house for the first time, he replayed every single happening. When he got to the memory of searching Dr. Thompson's house, he stopped. Something hadn't seemed right with that certain aspect of the case. If he had seen them coming, he would have had to go out the front door to escape, in which case they would have seen him.

Unless there was a back door.

Smith opened his eyes. They had all been so rushed to curb their hunger that they hadn't thought of the possibility of another exit for him to take. Detective Smith put his car into Drive and headed to the house of Dr. Wilson Thompson.

Back inside the living room of Dr. Thompson's house once more, Smith started taking in every single. Nothing seemed to have changed since his last visit. He searched the kitchen but found no evidence of a back door or a secret entrance. The living room and upstairs yielded the same result.

Hmm, maybe I need to start from the end instead of the beginning.

Once again, Smith was outside, driving in the rain. He started to circle the house in an effort to find what he was looking for. On the complete opposite side of the house, he found a single window.

It is too high for anyone to climb onto from the ground, but there was only one window in the house: the upstairs window. No other window could be found. Except this one. He must have had a way for him to get up there.

Smith walked a few feet forward and heard his foot clang on metal. When he looked down, all he could see were leaves. Clearing the makeshift camouflage revealed a ladder. Smith put the ladder up to the window and climbed up it.

Perhaps the window will be open.

Smith's thoughts confirmed the condition of the window. He opened it and crawled through it. A step ladder had been placed, connecting the window to a small room. Inside the room was all the evidence needed to convict Dr. Thompson for the crime. On the only table in the hidey-hole sat the only syringe that could have made the mark on Mr. Verner. Under the syringe were detailed charts and graphs showing combinations of different chemicals and medicines. On another sheet of paper, there were handwritten notes recounting the outcomes of the different combinations. Pinned against the wall was a schedule telling when and where Mr. Savage could be located during the past week. One date on the calendar was circled in a dark-red ink. The day that Mr. Savage lost his fortune.

If this is not enough to convict him, then I do not know what is.

Crumpled up on the floor was a small slip of paper. After unfolding it, Smith noticed that it had been torn from a larger piece of paper. The half that he had read Lincoln Hotel. He searched the room for the other half but to no avail. Smith was in the process of traveling back up the stepladder when his foot slipped, causing it to shift position. He caught himself before he could tumble down. While picking up the ladder to return it to its position, he noticed a tiny slip of white that was previously hidden. He took it into his hand and found that it was the missing half. Connecting the two yielded the words Lincoln Hotel 451.

It must have slipped out of his pocket when he was climbing out.

He returned the step stool and climbed out of the hidden room. Smith called the chief and told him that all the evidence he needed to convict Dr. Thompson was behind his house, up a ladder. After doing so, Smith pointed his car in the direction of the Lincoln Hotel and prepared to close the book on yet another case.

THE CONFRONTATION

Detective Smith stood alone outside room 451 of the Lincoln Hotel, readying himself for whatever was to happen behind it. Taking a deep breath, he opened the door. Smith found himself staring at the back of a tall, broad-shouldered man. He was bent over, engaged in some activity.

"Dr. Wilson Thompson?" The man turned around as quick as lightening at his name. Seeing whose face had addressed him, his expression turned into despair.

"I knew it was only a matter of time before you found me," Thompson said in a voice that had given up all hope.

"I take it that you know why I am here then?" Smith asked. The man before him gave a sad nod. Smith was about to continue whenDr. Thompson interrupted him.

"Before you go on, I just want you to know that my life has not been easy. I have made plenty of wrong decisions in my life, the worst being that I stole from my best friend." This comment was a surprise to Smith. "It has been eating me up ever since I did it."

"It sounds like you are willing to make a clean breast of it all," Smith asked.

"You are right. But how much do you know, Detective?" Thompson responded.

"From recent discoveries, I know that you have been planning this act for a while now. You enlisted the help of Mr. Tom Verner, so you could establish a timeline of Mr. Savage's whereabouts week by week. You used him because you were most likely feeling uneasy about what you were doing, and if you got caught, it would be the end to your plans. On the night before last, you put your plans to action. While Mr. Savage was sleeping, Mr. Verner snuck in, used a mixture of liquid nitrogen, a chisel, and a hammer to shatter the lock cleanly. Mr. Verner took out Mr. Savage's life savings and stashed them in the briefcase that he stole on your request. He then proceeded to the condemned building on a deserted street. You walked from the house into which you had recently moved to the rendezvous point. You bought the house because of its close proximity to the scene of the crime. Mr. Harting, who was looking for a quick pay raise because of his financial situation, held you up on the street. Being a kind-hearted doctor, you could not hurt an innocent bystander. Instead, you diverted his attention by throwing a rock against a car. It had the effect that you desired, making it easier to slip inside without being seen. Mr. Verner met you in the living room by a small table that he had positioned beforehand. He sat the briefcase on the table and demanded a percentage of it. You refused. In response, he drew out a pistol that he was concealing. A millisecond before the shot rang out, you misdirected the bullet, putting a hole in the electricity wires and taking out the lights. Once he was discombobulated, you put your invention to the test. You injected him with a combination of chemicals and medicines that would cause short-term memory loss. You wanted to make sure that it was as painless as possible. That is why you experimented on many types of injections, most of which can be found in your refrigerator. You used a chemical converter to acquire your homemade chemical that could produce the effect that you wanted. I have seen the charts and graphs in your secret room, and I must say that I am quite impressed. But sometime during your experiments, you fumbled what you were working on, scalding your hand and searing the chemicals into your carpet. Under that glove are probably fierce chemical burns. That is why you acquired first-aid supplies. Anyway, after eliminating your accomplice, you grabbed the briefcase and went on your way. We happened to be eating at the same restaurant as you, which, no doubt, made you paranoid, causing you to run to your car, drop a certain incriminating one-hundred-dollar bill, and speed off, leaving tire marks in your wake. Fearing that we could track you by means of your car, you abandoned it on the side of the road. It slipped your mind that you had put the briefcase in the glove compartment until after you had dropped you car off. You ran over to the passenger side and got the briefcase. But what you did not realized was that the passenger side of the car was covered with mud. While you were getting your briefcase, you tracked mud into the car, negating your original intentions. Fearing that your home was no longer safe, you fled to a predestined place. The very room that we are standing in now," Smith concluded. Dr. Thompson had sat in silence during the detective's speech.

"You are spot on, Detective. There is just one point that you are in the dark on,"Dr. Thompson said.

"What is that?"

"Do you know why I took the money?"

"That was one of the points I was going to ask you," Smith answered.

"The reason I did it was because I was failing as a provider. I have a family that needs me to always be there, Detective. How can I be there when I am working for a doctor who uses the money that he gets to enhance his appearance to others? On top of that, I am in the middle of a lawsuit that is not my fault, but since the other guy can afford to pay a better lawyer than me, I will probably end up paying him a lot of money. My best friend comes across that much money, and I could not resist. He had already told me about his briefcase that was layered with lead and his vacation tickets. I found out about the money checking the listings of houses he was selling. I did the math and figured that he had money, and I needed money. And seeing as how I am not going to get the chance to use it…" Dr. Thompson explained, snatching up the item he was fiddling with and handing it to Smith. The detective quickly opened it and saw numerous stacks of bills gleaming back at him.

"So you planned to hide the money in the briefcase, and since it had a lead covering, it would scramble the x-ray image when it went through security and look like something else."

"Spot on, Detective."

"You should know that even if you were able to get into the airport, there is a squad of policemen waiting there to apprehend you," Smith said.

"Either way, I was trapped," Thompson said with finality. After this statement, there came a loud bang at the door.

"Dr. Thompson, we have a warrant for your arrest!" the voice of the chief yelled. The man in question walked to the door and opened it for the police. The chief motioned for an officer to handcuff him. He noticed Smith standing a ways off. "Ah, Detective! I thought you would be here. What did he say?"

"Made a full confession, Chief," Smith said, passing the satchel to him.

"Really? Good. This one is going to be pretty cut and dry. Just the way I like 'em," the chief said.

"Me too," Jefferson said, coming into the fray.

"Do you think that he will confess in front of a jury?" the chief asked the detective.

"I have no doubt in my mind. He was content enough to tell me the whole story, and he will do it again."

"Even if he doesn't, we have enough evidence to convict him."

"I can't believe we were standing on top of it all that time," Jefferson said.

"We still got to it, thanks to the Detective," the chief said. The officer that had handcuffed Dr. Thompson had finished reading him his Miranda Rights and had begun to escort him down to a police car.

"What exactly did he say?" Jefferson asked.

"Come over after you have booked him, and I will explain everything. I need to pay you two back for dinner anyways," Smith said.

"Sounds like a plan to me," Jefferson said.

"I second that. Catching criminals makes me hungry," the chief agreed.

THE HUNT CONTINUES

A few hours after Detective Smith had explained every aspect of the case to the chief and Jefferson, he sat down at his desk to finally finish his letter. He signed his name and set it aside for when he had time to visit the post office. Smith had one hand reaching for his coffee when a knock emitted from his door. He opened it to find Mr. Savage standing on his threshold.

"Hey, Detective. I just wanted to thank you personally for getting me my money back," he said. Smith noticed that he looked like a new man already. The eternal exhaustion that Smith had sensed around him now was gone. He appeared to be twice more energetic than he had been as of late.

"It was my pleasure, Mr. Savage. Come on in!" Smith said, motioning for him to take a seat.

"At least now, I don't have to worry about getting your floors soaked," he commented. The endless rain had finally ceased to exist in the air. Smith noticed how much a simple change in weather could affect people.

"What have you done since you got your money back?"

"I figured that a bank account was much more secure than a safe at my house, so I put my money in one. Now I can watch over it whenever I want," Savage said.

"I am glad."

"Me too. I was shocked to find out that my own best friend was the one who stole from me. I never expected that he was the one who stole my briefcase. He never even crossed my mind as a suspect. I guess it's all over now, though. But I went down to the police station with his family, and he explained the whole thing to me. I offered to give him some money, but he said it would be useless considering he is going to be spending the next several years in prison."

"Since he confessed, he might possibly get some time knocked off," Smith said

"Possibly. Anyway, Detective, thanks once again for giving me my life back. I sure owe you one. Now, if you excuse me, I have a business deal to close," Savage said, getting up, shaking the detective's hand, and walking out the door. Smith, after grabbing the letter, followed suit.

Detective Smith pulled into the police station's parking lot on a mission. When he walked in, he was greeted with more than the usual salutes from officers.

"Well done on solving yet another case, Detective!" the receptionist said once Smith walked up.

"Thank you. But I could not have done it without the help of you guys."

"It was our pleasure, Detective! If you ever need anything at all, do not be afraid to ask!"

"Actually, I was wondering where I might find the chief."

"At the moment, he is interviewing Dr. Thompson in his office. He has quite a lot to say," the receptionist commented.

"Thank you once again." Detective Smith made his way to the chief's office. On his way, he ran into Jefferson who was talking to Mr. Savage.

"I heard that you helped quite a lot in the investigation to get back my money, and I wanted to thank you with this before I left," Mr. Savage was saying to the deputy. He reached into his wallet and pulled out the Where's Benjamin? that had been a breaking point in the case and handed it to Jefferson.

"I can't accept this..." Jefferson mumbled.

"Go on take it! Without you and the chief's help, I might not have my money back," he concluded as he smiled at the detective and left the station.

"I cannot believe this... I have a real Where's Benjamin?" Jefferson looked as if he was about to faint.

"Excellent job on the case, Deputy Trueman," Smith said, shaking the young man's hand. Jefferson mumbled something inaudible, still transfixed at his newest prize. Detective Smith opened the door to the chief's office where he and Dr. Thompson were having a conversation.

"I understand the reason behind your actions, but the law is still the law. You broke it, so you must be punished accordingly," the chief said.

"I understand, Chief. Thank you for your time," Dr. Thompson said, as he turned to leave. On his way out, Smith stopped him with a question.

"One more question, Dr. Thompson. Why did you send someone to my house last night?" A look of utter confusion came over the man in front of the detective.

"What do you mean? I haven't talked to anyone ever since my crime," he said as an officer walked him out. Smith could see absolute truth in his eyes.

"Detective, this means that your attacker went to your house under different orders. What now?" the chief said slowly.

"The hunt continues," Detective Smith said as he situated his coat and walked out the door.

ROUND TWO

The Third Adventure Recorded
By Detective Smith

THE TRIO

The rays from the hot, midday sun beat relentlessly down upon the three prisoners as they worked feverishly to clean a deserted section of land away from the main highway. These three men knew each other well, given the fact that they had been grouped into the same work force for nearly five months. Two guards had been assigned to the trio of detainees to look after any and all activity that came into contact with them. These guards had become so accustomed to the presence of the culprits that they became less strict than they might have been had the guards' positions changed every now and then. While the prisoners worked, the two guards nonchalantly kept an eye on them while chatting about various aspects of their lives. If they had been a little more attentive, they might have noticed that one of the prisoners strayed from his designated zone toward another one of the trio.

"You are a little far from your designated area, Sledgehammer," the man commented as the other man walked over to him. The man's nickname was a direct definition of his physique. From far away, one could easily mistake him as a small mountain. Ever since he had been detained, he had been building up his muscle mass little by little until he was twice the size of the man before him.

"They won' notice," Sledgehammer said, indicating the oblivious guards. The other man took a quick glance then continued on his work.

"True. So much could go unnoticed before their very eyes."

"My point exactly. The time is ripe," he said, his Scottish accent bleeding through in his excitement.

"We will require the ears of Informant if we are to make a move."

The one nicknamed Sledgehammer looked across the grassy area to his other companion. "Three o' us in one place might draw attention," he said warningly. The other man thought for a moment, contemplating their situation.

"Tell Informant to be ready to move at a moment's notice. Once put in motion, it will be impossible to stop."

"All right. Anything you need me to do, Mastermind?" Sledgehammer asked.

"I do believe that it is time to put your casting arm to the test," Mastermind said with a slight smile, pointing to a large rock a little ways off. Sledgehammer returned the smile and strode off to take his position. Once he had gone, Mastermind looked over his targets. He noticed that the two guards had produced a deck of cards in their boredom and were trying to outdo one another with poorly done card tricks. Feigning exhaustion, Mastermind gave a groan loud enough for the guards to hear. One of them gave a sigh to the other and proceeded to walk over to investigate.

"Everything okay over here?" he asked in a monotone.

"I-I'm exhausted. I can barely stand. You…you have got to help me." Mastermind exhaled heavily. The guard regarded him with an uninterested expression as he raised the Coke in his hand to his lips. "Please… just a few minutes of rest." Seeing that he could barely form sentences, the guard decided to take advantage of the situation.

"I'll make you a deal. If you can do a better card trick than me, and that also involves correctly finding my card, then I will take your place for five minutes. I will even let you drink the rest of my Coke," the guard said. "But if I win, you go to the head guard and tell him what a great job I have done and that I deserve a promotion for my efforts."

"But…but I don't know any card tricks," Mastermind stammered.

"Then you better get back to work."

"Wait…wait! I'll take the deal," he called once the guard had taken a few steps away from him. The guard smirked and pulled out the worn deck of cards. He shuffled them and performed a simple trick, correctly guessing his card. Once the deck was in his hands, he shuffled them poorly, raising even more the guard's confidence. Once the guard had chosen a card, Mastermind pushed all other thoughts from his mind. He separated the cards into four piles and shuffled them using an old trick he had invented. He brought the bottom cards from one pile onto the top of the next, then did the opposite with the other decks, shuffling them so fast that the guard's eyes could not keep up. To add more grandeur to the trick, Mastermind threw up one of the decks and snatched a card out of mid-air.

"Is this your card?" he asked. For an answer, the guard grumbled under his breath and shoved the Coke toward the prisoner. Mastermind stepped aside and let the guard take up his post. While this was going on, Sledgehammer had completed his part of the deal, leaving an unconscious guard in his wake. Informant had joined Sledgehammer in collecting the unconscious guard's provisions. Recognizing this, Mastermind knelt down and deposited a hand full of grass and dirt into the aluminum Coke can. He gave the working guard a slight tap on the shoulder. When he looked up, Mastermind threw a concoction of Coke, dirt, and grass directly into the guard's eyes. The guard doubled over in pain, falling to the ground in his agony. Once the pain had subsided, he looked up just in time to see the last distant silhouette disappear into the cover of the nearby forest.

The three escapees collapsed exhaustedly next to a large log for a moment's rest. The darkness of the night was intensified even more by the closeness of the trees to such an extent that they could barely tell each other apart.

"Tha' should be far enough," a deep voice breathed tiredly from the dark.

"I agree," a more alert voice said. The owner of the voice took a quick inventory of their situation. "Informant, I trust you know what steps to take next?"

"Yes."

"And you will not fail us?" Mastermind questioned severely.

"Don't forget that I have a score to settle as well."

"Very good. After you have accomplished your task, I expect for you to be at the location that I specified to you. Do not be late. Understood?"

"I understand."

"Then we are done here. Let's move, Sledgehammer. We have till morning until they find out that three of their most well behaved prisoners have gone missing." Mastermind said, motioning for the large man to follow him.

"Take this. Bein' on the run isn't easy. Good luck," Sledgehammer told Informant, tossing him a backpack filled with provisions, then following the other man into the shadow. The remaining prisoner hefted the backpack over his shoulder and revealed a newspaper clipping dated last month. The headline read The Police Department and Det. Smith Are at It Again! An article of impressive length followed the title, but only two words held the prisoner's eyes.

In a dark-red pen, the name Det. Smith was circled. He crumpled up the small piece of paper and threw it on the ground. As he turned to leave the clearing, one thought was plastered deep in his mind: *You will not escape me.*

A START TO THE INVESTIGATION

Detective Smith stared intently at the amount of leads and trails that had accumulated over the past month. He had converted his office desk, which was located in his living room, into a file cabinet for just these things. The stack had gotten so large that Smith had trouble keeping tabs on the many clues that had come into his possession. Ever since the knowledge that the attempt on the detective's life was not related to the case involving Dr. Wilson Thompson, Smith had slowly and methodically traced the steps linking the hitman to himself. The result was a multitude of different theories regarding the crime. Detective Smith had enlisted the police department's help in the matter so as to cover more ground. As in most of Smith's cases, the department took up the challenge with zeal. The weeks following the merging of the town's two most reliable assets yielded no result. All the trails that the detective had taken up all ran cold, no two of the links fitting into the same chain. The men from the police HQ soon noticed this also.

Couple that with the fact that crime never sleeps, and most of the policemen were reluctant to continue on their current course. The chief inspector was the single individual who never gave up on the hunt. His mind was thrust away, however, from the investigation by a sudden outbreak of crime. Thus, Detective Smith found himself fighting a slowly losing battle alone. But in spite of all the evidence, his perseverance had not run dry. From his searching, he had brought a few facts to light. Whoever had sent the hit man after him was highly skilled in the art of deception. His familiarity with the detective's system of investigating was exact and timely. He possessed a sufficient amount of facts about the case and how it was progressing to know that the prime moment to strike was during the moment when suspicions were highest toward another culprit. Detective Smith was pondering these aspects when the ringing of his cell phone broke through his trance.

"Hello, this is Detective Smith... Ah, Chief! How have the past few weeks treated you? Yes, I noticed that in the newspaper... I must congratulate you on another job well done. I have noticed long ago that luck has very little to do with finding a solution to a crime when a skilled investigator as yourself is behind it... To what occasion do I owe this honor? Uh-huh... I will be there as soon as I can, Chief." Detective Smith hung up his phone, grabbed his coat and headed out the door to another adventure. The chief had called from the state penitentiary a few miles outside the city limits. Upon arriving there, Smith noticed that many of the guards were agitated and on high alert. The chief found the detective the minute he stepped out of his car.

"Perfect timing, Detective," the chief inspector said, giving Smith's hand a firm shake.

"It was my pleasure, Chief. After all, you were one of the very few people who continued on my very unprofitable investigation."

"You might want to reconsider that."

Smith gave a curious look to the chief's remark. "You believe the two are related?"

"Considering the circumstances of the crime, yes, I do," the chief answered with a nod.

"The crime being that three detainees managed to escape their two guards and are now on the run?"

The chief gave a questionable glance at this analysis. "How did you know that?"

"According to the state penitentiary rule book, two guards are to be assigned to every three prisoners. I observed as I drove up that you had concluded a conversation with a guard. A layer of dirt and grass can be seen on the guard's shoes. This indicates that he had been doing work detail with a trio of criminals because the ground that the prison lays on is too hard to adhere to the surface of the shoe. The other guard, I presume, is being treated for wounds that he sustained while the escape was in progress," Detective Smith concluded.

The chief looked at him with amazement. "You never cease to amaze me, Detective. You are spot on. Three criminals escaped from their two guards around noon yesterday. I was notified this morning. Once I learned of the situation, I called you."

"Do we know the names of the three escapees?"

"I sent Jefferson a while back to see what he could find out about the prisoners, names included," the chief said, checking his watch. As if on cue, the deputy of the police department exited the prison and walked over to the two men.

"Hey, Chief. I questioned a good amount of the guards, and they couldn't give any facts about our runaways. I even turned toward the other prisoners. But they didn't know one thing about them. It's as if they do not exist. Except for the fact that they managed to disable two guards and escape," Jefferson said, not looking up from his notepad.

"So the three prisoners that everybody knows the least about have gotten away. Perfect," the chief said, rubbing his temples with both hands. Jefferson looked up to comment and took notice of the third party.

"Boy, am I glad to see you, Detective!" he said with a large exhale. "I can't make heads or tails of it! We practically have them already arrested now that you are here!" He shook hands eagerly with his role model.

"I will help in whatever way I can," Smith answered. He then turned to the chief. "What clues do we have regarding their escape?"

"Not much. Whoever they were, they certainly know how to leave a clean crime scene. Still, I had my men not touch anything until you had a good look at it."

"Why, thank you, Chief! It is not often that one gets a fresh look at things."

The chief led Jefferson and the detective over to his car. "It's a little bit out of the way, so we will need to drive," the chief said, motioning his car in the process. The three of them got in and proceeded down the dirt path that led out of the prison.

"Why do they build prisons way out in the middle of nowhere? It seems to me to be a free ticket to escape," Jefferson asked, staring at the large tracks of uninhabited land that passed by.

"If they built it close to town, the residents might get nervous at having a large amount of convicts next door," the chief responded.

"Makes sense." The conversation died off until the chief pulled his car to a patch of land that was no different than the rest.

"This is the location where our convicts made their escape?" Smith asked, shutting the car door behind him.

"This is it," the chief answered. A quick survey of the land told that this was an ideal place to make a getaway. The land was practically flat with a few bulges here and there. Roughly a quarter of a mile off was a dense forest that spanned the majority of the horizon. Only one object stuck out in the vast expanse of green. Two chairs were perched in a seemingly random location off to the side. Smith set his attention on these and walked over to them. It was evident that this was where the two guards took up their post. A can of Coke was crushed and thrown to the side of one of the lawn chairs. A plastic wrapper of sorts also found its home among the post.

"Doesn't look like they were very attentive," Jefferson said, walking over to where Smith was examining the site.

"Based on what the guard that I questioned said, I have to agree with you," the chief commented, joining in.

"Given the fact that the exact same pair of guards are given the exact same trio of convicts, I would wager that they were so accustomed to their presence that they did not feel the need to keep a close inspection on them," Smith inferred.

"That corroborates with what the guard said when I questioned him on his conduct that day," the chief said.

"That would explain the Coke cans and the comfy chairs," Jefferson threw in.

"But even an inattentive prison guard would be able to tell when his prisoners were making an escape. We already have at our disposal the knowledge that somehow one of the guards became incapacitated, thus preventing him from intervening," the detective said.

"There was still one guard who could have done something when he saw that his partner was down," Jefferson thought aloud.

"Precisely. That means that an incident occurred that kept the second guard's attention away from the first guard."

"But what? The man I talked to didn't tell me anything and waddled off complaining about heat exhaustion when I threatened him with obstruction of justice," the chief asked, his mind having trouble disconnecting from the now and reconstructing the events that transpired in the past.

"That is what we need to find out." Detective Smith put himself in the guard's place by sitting in the chair nearest him. One of the most important aspects of investigation is the ability to set aside yourself and take on the identity of the person in question. This process allows you to determine the thoughts and actions of a different person, in turn producing the thoughts and actions of another, the other person, in this case, being the criminals. Smith looked out over the breadth of land before him. He adjusted his gaze to fit the height of the guard that he had observed talking to the chief. Once he had done so, he noticed the sun reflecting off an object residing on the ground a little ways off. Smith followed the reflection to the place where the object was lying. He knelt down and picked up the small item. Turning it over revealed a jester on a unicycle with the word "Joker" printed above.

"It looks like the guards got a little uninterested and decided to play some cards," the chief said, observing the small card in the detective's hand.

"But why are they so far away from the makeshift post?" Jefferson asked. Smith noticed that twelve other cards were lying in a pile to the left of the lone joker.

"What is the reason for a fourth of a full deck of cards to be apart from the rest?" Smith asked more to himself than to his companions.

"Maybe the guards decided to share with the prisoners," the chief commented, nodding toward another empty aluminum can.

"Possibly, but then, how would we account for the other three-fourths of the deck. The guard that you were engaged in a conversation with did not appear to be carrying thirty-nine playing cards on him," Smith explained.

"If they were on him, he might have had time to put them somewhere before being questioned," Jefferson said with a shrug.

"Since the crime was reported this morning and the guard in question was interrogated this morning also, there was most likely not a big margin of time for him to deposit the cards," the detective said, gazing down at the remainder of the deck. A large imprint off to the side caught his eye. The grass had been matted down in what appeared to be an enormous shoe print. The pattern continued to advance backward every two feet in a left to right sequence.

"It appears as though one of the three detainees walked over to this spot, leaving behind evidence of his actions."

"There were three convicts on work detail yesterday. That at least accounts for two of the three," the chief commented.

"Two of the three?" Jefferson asked.

"The guard that I questioned reported that the man who he talked to was of medium build."

"How does that account for the other criminal?" Jefferson pressed.

"The footprints themselves are very large, indicating a large owner to those shoes. In addition, they are imprinted every two feet. Using this measurement, we can determine that the convict is very tall and very well built," Detective Smith explained. A look of dawning comprehension came to the deputy's face.

"That is amazing. Where did you learn how to tell a suspect's height just from his shoe prints?" Jefferson asked.

"Every body movement can tell a story. The trick is sifting away which parts to that story are irrelevant. Using something as simple as a shoeprint can produce the image of the suspect in your mind, bringing you one step closer to your goal." Jefferson stared in rapt awe at Smith's deduction.

"That is why you are the best, Detective," the chief said.

"Not the best, Chief. Without the police department, I would not be where I am today," the detective responded. The chief waved away the comment as soon as it was given. He then turned his attention back to the tracks in front of him.

"So these footprints can account for two of the prisoners, but where is the third?" he asked to no one in particular.

"If all three of them escaped, shouldn't there be three sets of footprints?" Jefferson cut in.

"My thoughts also. Unless a situation arose where the three of them together would warrant attention to themselves," the detective said, thinking hard.

"Well, if all of my prisoners were all in one place, I would be suspicious," the chief said.

"I suggest that we follow the prints belonging to the larger man. From what is shown in the dirt, the first man never took a step away or toward the guards at their post." Detective Smith then proceeded to put his plan into action. With the chief and Jefferson close behind, he trailed the second track as far as it would allow. It came to a stop at the western most end of the plot of land, where a third set of prints was awaiting them.

"These are not as large as the ones we just saw, but larger than the first. So the third prisoner is a man of medium build and height," Jefferson said, putting into practice Smith's methods.

"Well done, Deputy Trueman," Smith said.

"All this still doesn't tell how they escaped," the chief said. The detective looked hard at the new set of tracks in front of him. A deeper impression to his right caught his attention. They looked almost identical to the tracks of the third man, but something was different. The toes of each set of tracks was deeper and more profound than the heel.

"They were running," Smith told the two beside him.

"Why did they wait so long to run? Why not take off once they realized that the two guards weren't looking?" Jefferson asked. This comment yielded a long silence from the detective. He thought about all the evidence that they had in their possession.

"It was not the opportune moment. They needed both officers to be completely oblivious to what they were doing," Smith said slowly. His eyes then drifted back to the two lone chairs sitting out of place on the flat expanse. A large rock that he had not noticed before was lying a few yards away from the chair on the right.

No one could throw a rock that size very far, especially at an angle. But what if it was not thrown at an angle?

Smith walked away from the tracks, keeping his eye on the rock at all times. He came to a halt when the rock was in a straight line with him. Looking down, he saw the footprints of the bigger man engulfing his own.

"What is it, Detective?" the chief asked.

"Notice how we are in a straight line with the rock." He pointed to indicate the object he was talking about. "We are standing directly on top of the location where the larger man would have been standing. A man of any other size would have had trouble throwing a rock that size that far. Also, the return tracks come to a stop at this position, indicating that he had an objective only after he returned," Smith explained.

"So the bigger man and the smaller man were planning out their escape?" Jefferson said, talking fast in his excitement.

"Precisely."

"But that only tells how one of the guards was taken care of. What about the other?" the chief asked, his mind just now catching up with the flow of clues.

"How indeed," Smith agreed slowly. He gazed once more to the spot where the third tracks were discovered. "We can entirely eliminate the third man for this instance. There are no significant clues telling that he was responsible for incapacitating one of the guards."

"The only other option is the first prisoner."

"Then therein lies the answer." Smith strode over to the beginning of the impressions, looking out for any clues. The only objects in sight were the few playing cards that were lying on the ground a few feet from where he was standing.

“We first saw the playing cards by the guard post, so we can assume that they were originally there,” Smith told the two men.

“How did they get all the way over here?” Jefferson asked. Detective Smith compiled all the information that they had recently acquired.

“This was a very elaborate escape plan, everything had to line up perfectly for it to commence. It required both guards to be immersed in the distraction that was played out. We have one method of distraction at our disposal, but what of the other?” Then it dawned on him: a card trick. Detective Smith scanned the ground at his feet for the sign that would confirm his theory. Kneeling down, he picked up a playing card that looked no different from the rest. The only difference on this card was that the bottom left corner was slightly peeled back. He held up the card for the chief and his assistant to acknowledge.

“One of the corners is bent back,” the chief commented.

“As if this card was the only one with significance,” Jefferson said.

“There is only one thing that I have knowledge of that involves an incomplete deck of cards and a singular card,” the detective said.

“A card trick,” the chief and Jefferson said simultaneously. Smith gave a slow nod. Silence followed while the three men pondered the mystery before them.

“How can a simple card trick con a veteran prison guard to the point of allowing his captives to escape?” Jefferson voiced the question that was on everyone’s mind. Detective Smith stood up with a determined look crossing his features. A quick glance at the chief told him that his thought process was mutual.

"This was no circumstance. The man who accomplished this escape was a master of diversion. It would required the mastery of the art of drawing your victim's attention away from what was truly going on by the use of complicated, intricate systems that look like the truth, but in the end, are nothing more then fallacies made up to fool the target." Smith said all this from the deepest shelves of knowledge in his mind. This profile had been locked away in the recesses of his brain for quite some time, not wanting to resurface.

"Sounds to me like whoever can use this skill can have the influence over nearly anyone," Jefferson responded.

"Every criminal has some ounce of this ability. It is what makes them think that they can get away with the crime that they have committed. Only a few great criminals truly have the full extent of this talent, if you can call it that," the chief said.

"How would one stop a criminal with that kind of ability?"

"It takes the full extent of the police force," the chief responded with conviction. Detective Smith was absorbed in thought during this exchange. There was only one human being with the power and knowledge to succeed in such an endeavor. All of the instances associated with this singular man rushed into his mind. His eyes locked with the chief. He could tell that the chief was coming to the same realization that he was. Smith watched his emotions turn from confusion to raw shock in an instant as the gravity of the situation came down on him with full force. The detective's attention was drawn toward the edge of the forest. One emotion slowly began to take control over all the rest in his mind. For the second time during his career, one emotion was present in every fiber of his being: fear.

THE BEGINNING OF A TRAIL

Two cars pulled quickly into the parking lot of the police headquarters. Detective Smith exited his vehicle, then proceeded to the parking space adjacent to his own. The chief inspector stepped out and made a course toward the large double doors that were the entryway into the four-story building. Silence accompanied the two men as they walked quickly into the HQ.

"Everyone is waiting for you, sir," the receptionist said to the chief, who returned this statement with a worn smile.

"Thank you." Detective Smith took notice of just how barren the police department was. Directly after his shocking revelation, the chief had immediately hailed his receptionist and told her to gather everyone in the conference room. Upon entering the large, cozy room, Smith observed that the entire senior-ranking members of every division were present. He saw the familiar face of Bernard, the most skilled man in the forensics department who was instrumental to solving his last case.

"We all know why we are here," the chief said, skipping the preamble. He made a quick motion for everyone to sit down before he continued. "Three prisoners from the state penitentiary escaped, managing to incapacitate their guards. As of right now, these three men are this department's highest priority. We need them brought in fast. Stop at nothing to apprehend them."

"Do we know the names of these men?" an officer in the front row questioned.

"No, we don't. One of the guards said that their files were destroyed in a fire about a week ago. The prison tried to cover it up because one of their men had caused it, so that's why it never hit the news. Pretty much the only thing we know is their body types," the chief responded.

"How do we know that but not their names?"

The chief gave a nod in the detective's direction as an answer. The quizzical officer sat up a little straighter and became silent.

"Bring these convicts in. This town doesn't need three convicted men running free. It's already one-thirty, meaning that these guys have an hour and a half on us. Let's not give them any more," the chief concluded. So accustomed to the chief's speeches, the whole assembly recognized the closing tone in his voice. In a matter of seconds, the many officers and experts were off to fulfill their duties.

"Great speech, Chief," Jefferson commented, walking over to him.

"It'll have to do. I just hope that we can catch them before they get too far. "Do not worry, Chief. We will get them," added Detective Smith. His dedication and perseverance was higher than ever for this case. The chief nodded in response.

"What's our next step?"

"It is critical that we find all we can about the perpetrators. If we know how they have acted in the past, then we can conclude where they are heading and what their objective is," Smith explained. "I think it is time to refer to Deputy Trueman for his report on the prisoners." Jefferson hurried to compile all the information he had gathered.

"There's not much of interest, Detective. All the prisoners that I talked to didn't seem to know anything about our guys. One prisoner that was a next-door neighbor to one of them said that they were model prisoners, never doing anything to break the rules. In fact, one of them only had about a month left to serve because of good behavior," Jefferson reported.

"Interesting," Smith said.

"If he only had a month left of jail time, then why bother to break out and risk adding more time?" the chief asked.

"Who knows?" Jefferson said, shrugging his shoulders.

"Well, Chief, it seems that we have found our first lead," the detective said enthusiastically.

"Any ideas that might give us a good starting point?"

"Something must have come up within the prison walls to merit this one convict to risk increasing his incarceration."

"I'll send a detail back down to the penitentiary to see if anything was going on that was out of the ordinary. Jefferson, do you have an urge to go back down there?" the chief said with a smile.

"They did not seem too fond of me, but if you need, I will go down there once more," Jefferson responded with his usually energy.

"Take a group of policemen and head there. You know the most about what is going on, and you have the most experience with the prisoners."

"Right away, boss," Jefferson answered, giving a quick salute. "Hope you find a lead yourself, Detective!" he called over his shoulder. The chief turned back to address Smith. Before he could give his statement, a young woman walked briskly to him.

"Sir, we've got a problem. Somehow a little whiff of what is going on has reached the press. I have tried talking with them, but they seem bent on figuring it out."

The chief gave a sigh to this statement. "I'll see what I can do. The last thing we need is for the public to be thrown into a panic. I just don't know how they always know about things like this." The woman gave a tired look and was about to walk away when she saw the detective.

"Hey, you're Detective Smith! I should have known that you would be on the case. I didn't see you during the conference because I was in the back. I bet your job isn't the easiest around."

"Everyone in the police department has a much more taxing job than I. Particularly a liaison like yourself. I respect the department immensely more because of it," Smith said with a smile.

"Being a liaison is tough. Wait, how did you know that I was a liaison?"

"When you speak, your tone is calm and collected. You neither convey anxiety or enthusiasm, a trait that is vital for your job. In addition, you came to the chief for advice. This conveys that you are the most skilled individual with the press than everybody except for the one person who has the most experience," Smith explained.

"That is some of the best analyzing I have ever seen. If we don't nail these guys, I will be shocked."

"I trust the abilities of those involved in solving this case. But be mindful that for every protagonist there is an equal antagonist with the same skill set as yourself," Detective Smith said.

"How do you know when you come across someone like that?" the liaison questioned.

"You know yourself more readily than anyone else. Only you can tell." The liaison left the chief and the detective with a thoughtful look on her face.

"Detective, it seems like we must part ways once again," the chief said.

"As always, when the plot thickens, we must grow apart," Smith said with a slight smile. They shook hands and the two men went their separate ways. Smith exited the HQ with an objective set in his head. It would be incalculably difficult to pick up the trail from where it last left off. The forest that the three men made their haven in would be too dense to make any headway as to where they came and went. He needed a whole new trail if he was going to shed some light on the situation. Detective Smith searched his mind over for any missed trails or leads that might have been overlooked.

It appeared that every single clue had been followed up in the initial investigation, leaving no lead unfinished.

This realization is only on the surface, however, Smith thought, beginning to peel back the outside layers of the case, *from what we have at our disposal, we can conclude that no substantial evidence was left behind at the crime scene. That is to be expected if he truly is involved. Then the only suitable lead is inside the culprits' very minds.* The detective pondered this fresh outlook. *The three escapees are the few people involved who know what the next step is. Therefore, by thinking what they think should yield their next step. Perhaps all of the attention is being thrust upon the one person who we know the most about. Taking him out of the equation leaves two other men who are as invisible and mysterious as ghosts. These other prisoners, by default, have to be people that he met in prison and became close to. No one who is breaking out of prison would accompany himself with two unknown men. Therein lies the clue.*

Detective Smith set his face into a mask of pure determination as he turned his car toward the one place where his suspect's name was most likely to be: the courthouse. Smith parked his car in the parking space closest to the courthouse and got out to admire the building. The regional courthouse was not an impressive building, unlike the police HQ. Besides a small sign, there were no indications that would differentiate it from the surrounding complexes. It was a small, one-story building with three different wings. The wing on the detective's right was the most recent addition and also was the object of his visit. The archives were put into place after a string of cases where two or more of the same people were involved in the same case. To save time for future references, the city council funded the new wing to be built. That way if there was a repeat offender on the stand, all the police had to do was pull the files. Detective Smith opened the two wooden doors and strode into the courthouse. Smith had only set foot in the courthouse one other instance in his lifetime. On both occasions, he was here for the same end result. Four years had done little to change the layout of the building. The first room that Smith came to was painted a dreary gray and tan color. Two doors on either side of the opposite wall lead to the two courtrooms that the structure housed. Smith diverted his attention away from these doors and walked down the westernmost hallway. Not a soul was in sight until he came to the entrance to the archives room. An overweight guard was present, but only physically. His mind was currently engaged on the two feet of sandwich that he was devouring.

"Excuse me," Smith said, shaking the guard from his sandwich-induced coma.

"Need to get in there?" he said with food in his mouth.

"My name is Detective Smith, and I believe that some files of interest are presently archived in that room."

"No kiddin'? Welp, here ya go!" The guard handed Smith the key to the room and went back to his massive sandwich. Smith was trying to shed some light on why the guard threw in a *p* at the end of his "well."

Appears that it will be a mystery that no one will be able to solve. He thought as he turned the key. An audible click was heard from inside the lock. The Archives Room was packed full of rows upon rows of files, all containing cases that went as far back as fifteen years. He walked to the nearest cabinet and pulled a file at random to acquire a bead on the time frame he was in. The time stamp at the top read October 22, 2010.

Hmm, I need to go back farther. Four years have elapsed since one of the most dangerous criminals I have come into contact with had been incarcerated. Based on the layout of the room, the most recent files are organized in the cabinets closest to the door for easy access. Meaning, that cases from four years ago would be a third of the way toward the back wall.

Detective Smith moved down the aisles until he was roughly a third of the way into he room. He glanced around at all the files that were accumulated in the year 2006.

I could sift through these files all day and yield no result. Without a lead, even if it is a miniscule one, to lead me, I have no feasible means of finding my man.

His cell phone started to ring, and he noticed the chief's numbered displayed in large numbers on the front.

"Why hello, Chief! Any news from the front? Uh-huh… Really? That is great! I knew it was a wise decision to send Jefferson… I foresee that he will be invaluable in this investigation… Chief, you are my saving grace. Thank you again, Chief!" Detective Smith silenced his end and gave a rare triumphant smile.

Jefferson had returned with a full report from the prison where the three culprits had escaped. Not much could be gleaned in the area of the escapees' names, but Jefferson had accomplished the next best thing: a nickname. One of the other inmates had heard someone refer to one of the missing as "Sledgehammer." This may be of no importance to many investigators and detectives, but from Smith's experienced eye, nicknames could be even more important then the actual name at times. It gave a look into the rare community that is established within a prison camp. Nicknames tell you how the other inmates felt about that particular person and, almost always, were a reflection of one aspect.

In this case, Sledgehammer could only be a reference to the man's physique. And it just so happens that there was a very large man who was part of the case at hand. Using this newly acquired information, Smith quickly scanned the files for the nickname Sledgehammer. On a hunch, the detective checked the cabinet that contained the entire *S* files. The third file that Smith pulled presented the information that he required. At the top of the cross-referenced file, the name Saunders "Sledgehammer" Macleod was printed in bold, black ink. Below followed a lengthy paragraph of all the compiled data about his case. Strangely, there was no picture to accompany the article. The Scotsman had been a very busy man four years ago. Four accounts of assault and battery were responsible for putting the man behind metal bars. Interesting enough, Mr. Macleod did not waive his right to a speedy trial. In fact, he recommended that the trial go as fast as possible and even suggested a time frame. Pleading guilty to all accounts did not help his case much either. Detective Smith stopped and thought about what he had read.

Why would someone who was going to plead guilty regardless not waive his right to a speedy trial? Any criminal who was on borrowed time would want to do everything possible to give him more freedom in my view. There is only one theory that explains all the facts that have been gathered. Mr. Macleod had to ensure that he was present in prison at the exact time because someone else was currently incarcerated that needed his attention and help.

Smith stood up as a shocking realization hit him. They had been planning this escape for four years. This comprehension yielded a new, equally puzzling question: Why not escape earlier? Why wait four full years? Taking one last glance and memorizing the finer details of the document, Smith closed the file and deposited it back inside the cabinet. He stood up and walked straight out of the archives room without letting any distraction penetrate his mind.

Detective Smith closed the wooden door to his home and casually tossed his hat on the hook. He had started frequenting an old-style bowler hat, one common to the late 1890s. He had procured it at an antiques shop and could not resist the urge to purchase it. The chief had remarked on it, saying that it "made the image of the detective complete." Ever since, it could always be found on his person. As he was pondering his wardrobe, his home phone rang. Smith glanced at the number for two rings before picking it up.

"Hello, this is Detective Smith speaking." Silence answered him in return. He checked and made sure that the call was still ongoing. As the call time hit thirty-five seconds, the call was abruptly dropped. Hanging up the phone, he cast his mind out to try and ascertain who was on the other end. No one usually called him besides potential clients and the chief. He gazed at his phone again and a thought struck him. *Thirty-five seconds is roughly how long it takes to copiously trace a call to the origin.* There was only one person in Smith's mind currently that would want to find out where he was located. And he was not a good guy. The detective thought it best not to tell the chief. It would only add more to his already full list of things to worry about. Smith would see to the issue personally. Smith did, however, need to get the chief up to date on his investigation. Just as with other cases that demanded much of his time, he remarked upon the somber fact that he is rarely ever home as he grabbed his hat and headed out the door. By now, Smith knew the police department like the back of his hand. He did not need to be told where the chief's office was in the large four story building. He registered briefly that the HQ was barren as he entered the chief's office.

"Ah, Detective!" the chief said walking up behind him. Smith turned to face him and noticed that he didn't have his usual confident gleam in his eye. To tell the truth, he looked almost nervous.

"Chief, is everything all right?"

"To be honest, Detective, I'm anxious to get this dirtbag caught. The first time around was bad enough."

"The first time around?" Jefferson poked his head in from around the corner, obviously intrigued at his boss's words. The chief and the detective locked eyes, silently agreeing whether or not to tell Jefferson about the threat at hand.

"Jefferson, you need to know the history of this guy before we get too deep in this," the chief said gruffly.

"The history? Boss, do you mean to tell me that you have seen these convicts before?"

"Not convicts, convict. Just one of them." Jefferson raised his eyebrows and set himself in a nearby seat.

"What did this guy do?" The chief followed suit and set down in his own chair. Detective Smith remained standing.

"His name is Neil Conway. He was, and still is to date, one of the most successful con men of the century. His skill at manipulation is unbridled. If he wants something, there is little anyone can do to stop him from attaining it. Most of his work was done in secret, slowly using his talents to acquire alternate identities and money, never leaving enough substantial evidence to convict him. Whenever one identity became heated, he shifted to another, once again disappearing off the sites of those hunting him. Art theft is also one of his strong points. He generally works alone. But in the case of the Gardner Museum heist of 1990, he had a partner. This particular case went unsolved, and to the knowledge of those involved in the investigation, it still remains so. His modus operandi lays in the fact that there is never enough evidence to establish a reliable modus operandi. Thus, there is no way to predict what his next step will be," Detective Smith explained. Jefferson analyzed and processed this information in the span of a few minutes.

"How do you know all this, Detective?" he said in awe. Smith gave a weary, age-old smile.

"Officer Trueman, the case of Mr. Neil Conway was the first investigation that launched my very active career. A few small clients had come to me for various reasons, but this was the focal point of four months of my life." Jefferson looked aghast at this news. This was quickly replaced with pure, raw amazement.

"So you were the one responsible for putting him behind bars in the first place?"

"That was the most curious event of that whole case. After months of tracking and following his trail, it led me to this very town. The things that he accomplished in my hometown were just a foreshadowing of what was to come. Equipped with the knowledge that his next play would be here, I proceeded to move with him and keep an eye out for any suspicious activity. In the process, I met none other than the chief, who was also on the lookout." The chief nodded at this statement. "It was just ripples at first, small whisperings of even smaller problems that seemed to have no significance. But to the chief and I, these were the first warning signs. Over the next few months, we noticed that nearly half the businesses in town were not acting the way that we knew them to. Upon further investigation, we pieced together the frightening fact that the majority of the stocks of all these said companies were stockpiled and obtained by the same man but with different aliases.

He was targeting the police Headquarters when that same HQ started to take action. With so many personnel on the lookout, the general thought was that he would not be a free man much longer. A few weeks passed, and people started to get nervous. The businesses that were taken over began to threaten the other "free" companies. But then one day, something peculiar happened. Neil Conway used his real name. This, as to be expected, caused a surge of action, and on the day he was caught and behind bars, I was the one who pinpointed his location and was the last one who spoke to him before his capture," Smith finished.

"Wait, if he was so analytical in his other crimes, why make so simple a mistake as using his actual name?" Jefferson questioned.

"That is the curious part of that case. It draws the question, did he truly get caught, or was that part of his plan all along?" Everyone in the room was silent at this remarkable statement. The unasked observations remained in the air, so evident that they need not be mentioned. Why did he get himself caught? What is his plan now that he escaped?

"Detective Smith, you caught this criminal once. If there is one thing that I know for certain, it is this: no criminal can escape you," the chief said with finality.

"Chief, I did not catch him. We did. As I have mentioned on more than one occasion, I could not imagine my cases without the helpful hand of the police department," the detective said with a gleam in his eye. Jefferson stood up and looked at the two of them hard.

"Chief, Detective Smith, we *will* catch this man." His statement seemed to reinvigorate the chief.

"Right you are, Jefferson! Detective Smith, what can we do? You have the most experience on this, more than anyone else here in this room," the chief said, his old energy returning to him in a tidal wave. Smith recounted the information he had acquired at the court archives in as much detail that he could remember.

"He didn't waive his right to a speedy trial? Hmm," the chief commented.

"I think your assessment that he had to meet someone in prison is right on the dot, Detective," Jefferson said with a nod of his head.

"Thank you, Officer Trueman. The only current problem is that we have no knowledge of where they are now. We know the identity of two of our culprits. If we can ascertain who the third is, we will have made a great contribution to the case."

"I'm not sure that the archives will help us. From my research at the prison, Sledgehammer was with our man nearly from the beginning of the four-year stretch. The other man was just recently seen in the group," Jefferson recited.

"Pulling files at random doesn't seem like the best course of action at the moment," the chief concurred.

"I tend to agree with you. Let's focus our attention on their meeting place. Every escapee has one, and I would hazard a guess that these men are no different," Smith said.

"I'll get my analysts right to work."

"An APB, boss?"

"Let's try just a general search of the adjacent area of the prison camp. After traveling all night through a forest, I reckon that they wouldn't want to travel too far."

"Yes, sir!" On his way out of the office, Jefferson turned back toward Smith. "Want to come with us, Detective? We could use your expertise."

"Lead the way." Smith had only been in the analyst's operating room once in the past. The two operators, Dan and Rick, had been very helpful on his last big case. The room was located on the third floor. After passing the first room on the right, the three of them entered through a small door. Nothing visually had been altered. All the same servos were up and running. Smith learned on his last visit that all the information that comes through the HQ is stored in this room. The most recent data was filed in the servo with the most available space on its hard drive, making for a relatively organized system. The two operators where sitting behind a brand-new desk with stacks of raw information surrounding them. At the closing of the door, they looked up. Dan and Rick exchanged a few pleasantries before getting down to business.

"What brings you three to our humble abode?" Dan asked excitedly.

"As you know, we are tracking the three convicts that escaped the state penitentiary. We need you and your partner to bring up a map and plot all the buildings that are within close proximity to the prison," the chief quickly explained.

"Ah, trying to find their meeting place, eh? We will get right on it." Rick already had a map up and was hammering in coordinates before the chief had even finished his sentence. In another minute, a large, detailed map was visible from his screen. To add dramatic flare to his performance, he flung his hands up in the air and spun in his chair to smile mischievously at the others.

"And that is why the forensics department has no chance of breaking the record that me and Dan set." Dan and Rick did a quick fist bump before continuing on. "Well, here ya go. Those are all of the buildings in a ten mile radius of the prison." The prison was centered on the screen with five small buildings on random splotches of land around it. The mass of green that was the forest spanned to the northwest of the prison.

"So what do you guys think?" Dan asked. Detective Smith glanced over the monitor.

"I must commend you on your speed. It seems like it has gotten faster since my last visit." He then pointed to the two buildings toward the south of the prison camp. "These two buildings here will not yield much. The prisoners escaped via the forest. They would have to backtrack all the way back to the penitentiary then proceed to trek to those buildings." Rick quickly cleared the two buildings in question off the screen.

"Can you plot the ones that are farther north? I feel like they would almost choose a building closer to the end of the forest rather than the beginning," Jefferson interjected.

"Your wish is my command." Within seconds, the view changed, now showing the dense forest in its entirety. One new building appeared at the far end of the left side of the forest.

"That's more like it. That building is way closer to the exit. That's where I would go if I were a convict," Dan said, nodding like this was common knowledge. The chief immediately extracted his cell phone from his pocket and hit the number two.

"It's the chief… I need you to be ready to roll in three minutes. Get me a helicopter in the air in ten. Notify squads one through three. We're going after 'em. Tell them these coordinates." The chief then recited the numbers that were on the screen. "I'll give you more details when you get there." He replaced his cell phone and almost ran out of the door. Detective Smith couldn't shake a foreboding feeling. If only he knew that this was a foreshadowing of things to come.

THE SEARCH

Detective Smith had never known the chief to drive so fast. He took a glance in the rearview mirror and saw that Jefferson shared his thoughts. No conversation could be made during the drive from the HQ to the spot where the team was going to meet. The chief's face was a mask of determination and confidence. The speedometer was pushing ninety miles an hour when their objective was in sight. They had long since passed the prison camp, their goal being on the other side of the forest. The chief drifted to a stop on a barren gravel road. The instant that the car was in park, he jumped out to survey the scene. Hopping out of the car, Detective Smith took a quick assessment of their scenario. The first two buildings could be seen on the horizon with a dense mass of green as the backdrop. The forest looked much more imposing than it did from the small guard post miles back. The chief was once again on his phone, most likely wondering the whereabouts of his helicopter crew. The soft sound of helicopter blades beating against the air put ease to his mind. Two more patrol cars rolled up besides the chief's just as the crew landed the helicopter. The woman who was piloting the vehicle took off her helmet to better address the chief.

"All right, sir. I believe that we all are here. So what exactly are we doing here? You said it had something to do with the escaped convicts?" The chief shouted for everyone to gather round before beginning his briefing.

"We have reason to believe that the convicts who broke out of prison are in hiding in one of these buildings." He referenced the building by a wave of his hand in their direction. "The mayor wants these men caught as much as we do, so he went ahead and got together a warrant. We will split up into three separate teams. The detective and I will take a few men and search the farthest building on this side of the forest. Jefferson here will take another and search the other building. The rest of you are to follow the forest about another five miles. There should be only one small, vacant building in site. This is your target. Ms. Kenny here is going to patrol these three spots and look to see if anyone comes out of them. Good luck and happy hunting."

The three squads broke off into separate groups. The team charged with the task of searching the farthest building got in a squad car and took off for the location. Jefferson gave a quick good-bye and drove off with his squad to his assigned building. The drive to the last building did not require much time. The chief parked the car a few hundred yards away so as to approach it quietly. After a few minutes walk, they were at their objective. The chief's men stacked up all around the doors while the chief and Detective Smith covered the front.

"Police, open up!" No one answered the chief's summons. He held up his hand and counted down from three. Once his hand was down, he then tried the door. To his dismay, the door opened smoothly. He quickly checked every room for signs of life. Smith, on the other hand, examined the entryway carefully, looking for any clues. Strangely, the whole house seemed to be spotless. Smith thought hard and finally struck upon the subconscious thought that was eating at him ever since the start of the search.

"Chief, they never used this house as a meeting place. I would also be willing to guess that we will not find any trace of them at the other locations either," Smith said slowly. In response, the chief pulled out his radio and inquired about the other teams.

"Nothing? Thanks, Jefferson… No, we didn't find anything either." He took a deep breath after clicking the off button on his radio. "No results with the other teams. Spot on, Detective. If he's not here, then where is he?"

"Most likely he predicted our moves before we even thought of them, Chief. After all, that is what his line of work requires." The chief nodded as the realization hit him.

"He knew that we were going to check the buildings that were the closest. That way, he could spend the extra time getting to one that was farther away."

"Precisely so." This short exchange was the only words spoken during the return trip to the police department. The chief gave a small announcement before returning to his car. Once back in his office, the chief sat down in his chair with a sigh.

"So he knew exactly what we were going to do and exactly when we were going to do it?" Jefferson asked in dismay. The chief gave a weary nod. Jefferson ran a hand through his hair with a look of shock and the tiniest amount of admiration written on his features. "So what do we do?"

"We follow the information that we already have. We are knowledgeable of the fact that one of his associates was present in the penitentiary at the same time that he was. Furthermore, it is safe to assume that the planning did not truly begin until the arrival of the third party. The questions that need to be answered are as follows: What could this third person contribute to the group that was not already provided? Solving this could give us the light we need to take the next step in this case," Detective Smith said.

"We'll get right on it, Detective," the chief assured with a confident smile.

"You can count on us," Jefferson agreed. Smith wished them luck and headed out to follow a separate lead of his own. During his short speech, an unanswered question fought its way into the forefront of his mind: Who was the mysterious caller that phoned his home? The detective could have easily gone up the elevator and reentered the analyst's office and politely requested that they track his line, but the chief would eventually get wind of his plan and would be on him in an instant. It just so happens that Smith knows of another person who can lend him a hand. And the fact that this person is unofficial is an additional bonus.

Once out of the police department, Detective Smith dialed the number of his friend Peter Connor. By an unexpected series of events, Smith ran into Peter Connor during a torrential rainstorm. Literally. After helping immensely solve his last conundrum, he had become a valuable asset and friend. The tone rang thrice before being answered.

"Mr. Connor, it's Detective Smith. Well, I have had a very interesting day to say the least. Yes, in fact, I have. I am calling you because I need your private expertise in the art of tracing calls from one location to its origin. I like to believe that I have an amateur skill at deducing. Yes, sir. I am on my way." Detective Smith long ago deduced that Mr. Connor had the means of tracing calls in addition to a complete forensics station in his very home. His connection to the forensics department came from his own skills at the trade. Detective Smith drove through a semicrowded street on his way to his friend's house. Mr. Connor's dwellings looked, in every way, absolutely normal. But a small bulge in the architecture betrayed the strangeness of the house. This addition was the office where Peter Connor did his work. The familiar face answered the door immediately at Smith's knock. One look at his friend told Smith that the past four months had been profitable.

"So, Detective, another tough case that you need to crack?"

"Precisely. I require your expertise once more, Mr. Connor. I hope that I am not interrupting an early dinner? "

"Nope, haven't even put it in the oven yet," Peter Connor said gesturing toward his office. His house was simple enough. The entryway was wider than long and opened up directly into his office. From the door, the makeshift forensics room was hidden just out of view.

The minute that Smith set foot into the dark room, he noticed a remarkable drop in temperature.

"Sorry about the cold. To get all the computers at maximum efficiency, the temperature has to be pretty chilly. They emit quite a lot of energy," Connor explained. Gazing at the small room, Smith could easily find the proof to back up his claim. The research and tracking equipment rivaled that of the analysts that Smith had just witnessed at work. Three monitors spanned the entirety of the face of the sturdy desk that he was using. Monitors twice the size of the surrounding ones were positioned at both ends of the chain. Built into the wall behind the screens was the computer itself.

"Detective, what do you need me to do?" Connor asked, prepping his systems for work.

"Previously today, I received a mysterious phone call. Upon retrieving the phone, I recognized that there was no one on the other end. After precisely thirty-five seconds, the other caller canceled his end," Smith described. Connor nodded his understanding.

"You want me to trace the call to find who the caller was. All right, Detective, I'll give it my best. I'm probably going to need your home number. I don't entirely trust my memory on seven digit numbers." The detective recited his number to the forensics amateur. Connor then copied the number to a blank line that appeared on his middle screen. He hit the Enter button and lists of numbers followed by Smith's own number filed down all five monitors. Connor stopped and concentrated, then hit a complicated series of keys. All the screens cleared except for two calls made to his home phone. The first number Smith acknowledged as the chief's. The second, however, was completely unknown. Connor opened up a command window and typed the words "trace all" into the engine. One after another the calls were highlighted, leaving an address after the task was complete. Smith dialed his mind in on the second address on the list. Using his extensive knowledge on the surrounding area, he constructed a map of the city with his mind's eye.

"That's peculiar. This call was completed from a small payphone on the outermost area of town," Smith thoughtfully said. Connor was silent a few moments as he thought out the detective's scenario.

"Detective, my advice remains the same as the last time that we talked about one of your cases. Try and see if you can find some fingerprints. Ever since that last case of yours, I have been working extensively on software that can process a fingerprint. I'm almost there, but I have to find a way into the police HQ's database. Might be a bit tricky."

"Mr. Connor, I will keep your advice readily in my mind as always. Thank you once again." As Smith was leaving, he turned to address his friend once more. "I wish you the best of luck on your steady flow of job offers that you have been receiving."

"How did you..." Connor said apprehensively.

"When you first allowed me into your home, I observed that you are wearing a brand-new suit. If you closely inspect the shoulder area, you will see the creases developed from the long curves of a hanger. No standard hanger has that certain design. Only hangers received from purchasing a new suit may cause depressions like that. This alone was not enough to enlighten me. But once I noticed the slight fading of several of your computer keys caused from a constant repeated action, in this case the action of tracing one's calls, it was evident. The act of tracing yielded a handsome reward, thus producing your suit," he explained. This produced a long and hard stare from the man in front of him. Thanking him once more, Detective Smith left Peter Connor's residence and made a beeline for the origin of the call.

The detective had rarely had an occasion to venture to the outskirts of the town. Unlike his other visits, he had an objective to follow. Mostly a quick passing through was the most that Smith ever saw of this small area of town. Dwarfed by the much larger surrounding sections of town, it slipped out of people's mind unbeknownst to them. The payphone that the call was traced to looked no different than the ones in the cleaner parts of the city. One glance told the detective that any chance of sweeping evidence off it were slim to none. The traffic that the phone must have would void any potential evidence. And since the identity of the caller was unknown, any and everybody could be considered a suspect. The aroma of the payphone wafted over him. He had to fight to tell his mind that he was not in the middle of a large dump. A strange orange substance was visible on the handle of the phone. Smith was determined to do whatever it took not to touch it. A soft cracking sound made him turn his head toward the row of houses on the other side of the rundown street. A man had just exited his house and was endeavoring to clean what was left of his yard. His foot making contact with a flimsy twig produced the noise. Smith noticed that his house was directly across from the small phone station and decided to see if the man had seen anything.

"Good afternoon. My name is Detective Smith. Would you mind if I ask you a few questions?" he said curtly to the man. He raised his eyebrows in a questioning manner.

"A detective, eh? Never heard of you." Smith marveled at the contrast between the area he had just come from and the block in which he now stood. He bent down to grasp another twig and took another look at Smith. "Sure, you can ask me whatever you like."

"Did you happen to recall any recent situations where someone used that pay phone across the street?" He looked up at the sky with a blank face,

"Yeah, actually. Only one person used it in the past twenty-four hours."

Smith's interest flared. "Is there any way you can remember what he looked like?" he prompted.

"Course I can. He just so happened to knock on my door." The detective had a hard time believing his luck.

"He was asking for money?" Smith wagered.

The man gave a snort. "Shoot, you really are a detective! Yup, he knocked on my door here and asked me for some change. He said he had to call someone and that is was important. 'It could be a matter of life and death,' he said. He was a rugged sort of fellow. Looked like he had seen some hard times. He was very polite when he asked for the money. I just had to give it to him, you know? Most of the time when people are trying to lie to ya, you can tell. But I could tell that this guy was telling the truth." Smith tried to direct the conversation back on course.

"Did this man happen to be wearing any suspicious clothing?" The man gave him an odd look.

"No, he just had on a dark jacket and jeans. He did have a backpack on his shoulder, though." Detective Smith had a strange inkling that the person that this man was describing was part of his current investigation. He decided to try the process of elimination.

"What was his physique like? Tall with an average build, or average height with an excess of muscle mass?" Smith questioned. The flow of questions was taking its toll on the man's memory. A whole minute passed before he responded.

"Definitely the first one. Yup. Cause I remember thinking that it would be a close match in an arm wrestling contest." So that eliminated that Scot from the line up. That left two more options: Conway or the mystery convict.

"Did you actually recall him using the change that you so generously handed him?"

"Mm-hmm. He kept it in his hand and then plunked 'em right into the payphone." Smith almost laughed out of satisfaction. A conman like Conway would not have such a haphazard plan of contacting him. And certainly would not have taken an innocent bystander's hard-earned cash and then proceed to spend it. Detective Smith extended his hand to the man.

"Thank you, sir. You have contributed greatly to my investigation." As he left the man's property, he saw out of the corner of his eye that his informant was standing a little straighter. Smith still had no way of tracking the third convict's whereabouts, but at least now, he had established who had called him. The objective of the call still remained a mystery. His only working hypothesis at the moment was that it was used to find out his location. In an ironic twist, the tracker had become the tracked. After the disappointment of the safe house search, this victory was much needed. A new thought process started in his head. As with every moment of jubilee, a fresh question was produced. If Conway was not after him, then who was? Comprehension on which escapee it was did not do much to answer the question of identity. The resources used for such a task had all been eliminated. The penitentiary, the court archives, and even the police station had all failed to retrieve the needed link.

Detective Smith made haste to inform the chief about his time spent in the outskirts. This was beginning to appear like a dangerous matter and Smith concluded it was time to relinquish his actions in regards to the investigation of the call. Only after the escape had the call come and the detective feared who might have been on the other side. While his thoughts drifted for the hundredth time toward Conway, he couldn't help but marvel at his skill. He had successfully tied off every loose end that would have betrayed him. Even going so far as to predict the police department's next move. The fear of him invading your mind and reading your thoughts was what kept him away from the arm of the law for so long. One deliberate mistake had the result of putting him behind bars for four years. Smith could only guess at the level of revenge that would cause. But why have revenge if you yourself were the reason why you accumulated your feelings of hatred. The cycle, both beginning and end, started with the same person. A thought hit Smith like a hammer.

Perhaps this was not about retribution. Perhaps it was a new round of dueling, a test of wits and deduction.

The vibration of Smith's cell phone caught his attention. His last thought before answering was, *How many instances has a caller intruded upon my thoughts?* The chief's number flashed up at him and he forgot about the annoyances his phone caused.

"In fact, Chief, I do have some interesting news. I have located, with the help of a local, the recent activities of what perhaps may be our missing convict. It is currently little more than a hunch, but hunches are, after all, the building blocks to information. My report can, however, wait. I do not want to bore you with conjecture. But based off the tone of your voice, I would say that you have had some success yourself… As would I, Chief… And, if I am correct in thinking, sensitive information would not be advised to give over the phone that I am currently using… What would be a suitable meeting place? I will be there shortly." Once the detective was back on familiar territory, he followed the echo of sirens until he arrived upon the seen of an arrest. The chief was standing talking to the press liaison once again. As Smith passed, she snapped off a crisp salute and continued to her duties.

"Just your everyday arrest, Detective. Caught smuggling jewelry out of Gemmed for Life again. I don't know what is with me and jewelry stores," the chief said, shaking his head. Jefferson emerged from the doorway leading a handcuffed man in front of him. He appeared, if anything, inconvenienced by the arrest as if it had interrupted a good movie he had been watching. He stopped abruptly by Smith.

"Hey! You're Detective Smith, right? Do you know any good lawyers? Mine kinda bailed on me last minute. What can you do, right? Yo, Jefferson, was it? Can you reach into my wallet and get out my card to give to the detective?" the criminal said happily. Curious, Jefferson took out one of the cards and looked at it.

"What kind of criminal has his own card? Chief, you have got to see this." He handed a card over to the chief. Over his shoulder, Smith read Steven Johnson, criminal grandeur. Address: Probably either (1) the courthouse, (2) jail, or (3) home. If number one, then find me a lawyer! The chief looked at Mr. Steven Johnson, criminal grandeur, with much confusion. Smith actually smiled after reading the small, laminated card. The handcuffed man shrugged good-naturedly before being hauled away into a squad car.

"At least, we will know where to find him," Jefferson commented after joining the chief and the detective.

"Chief, I believe that you and Deputy Trueman have some good news?" Smith initiated.

"It's more of a hunch, but we think it will help all the same, Detective. After leaving us with that question, we decided to get down to work. No sense in waiting around for the answer to fall into our laps. We attempted to take a leaf from your book and determine what each culprit had that the other didn't. Macleod, as we all should know, somehow hurled a boulder a good forty feet and knocked out a guard. Me and Jefferson here determined that his usefulness was his ability to do just that. Conway, on the other hand, has a good amount of knowledge and experience on how we work. And on top of that he is a con man. This, we think, is his contribution, a look into how we operate in addition to having the skill to plan this whole thing to the end," the chief finished.

"Excellently done! I have the utmost faith in your assessment," Smith said.

"What did you find out about the third convict, Detective?" Jefferson asked eagerly. The detective explained the mysterious call and the steps he took to pinpoint the location.

"I must apologize for the secrecy, Chief. I contemplated that if you knew about that call, it would have taken your attention away from other areas that it was needed in," Smith remarked.

The chief clasped him on the shoulder. "No need to apologize, Detective. We all have our ways of doing things around here."

"And if you did tell us about it, we probably would have been so engrossed in the call, that we would have forgotten about the third convict," Jefferson added.

"Well, Detective, I better head on back and make sure that Johnson is processed. Jefferson, make sure that he doesn't give his card to everyone he comes into contact with. And look into getting him a public defender. I have a feeling he won't object," the chief said, motioning Jefferson. As was custom when they parted ways, they all three shook hands. The chief and his deputy assured the detective that they would look into ways of finding out the next move of the third convict. Detective Smith still had a few tricks up his sleeve as well. After phoning his house, the mystery criminal would require a way to trace the phone number, exactly what Smith needed when tracing him. The similarity was not hard to miss. The convict's process had all the hallmarks of a detective's. The way that he talked to other people and received help from them was not unlike Smith's own process. The only difference being the thing given. The detective sought information to help him acquire his goal; the convict sought a few quarters to acquire his. Smith was expecting the convict's actions to be those of an amateur con man. This case had many odd twists and surprising turns, but one thing remained the same: Conway was not going to succeed a second time in controlling others. He may have knowledge on how he and the police department operate, but that blade cuts both ways. Sooner or later, Conway would make a mistake. And when he does, the detective is going to be right there to ensure that his mistake does not go unnoticed. The fox uses deceit and cunning to trap and devour its pray. Strip a fox of those two things, and it is weak and powerless. But a lion will always win out in the end, not matter the circumstances. Detective Smith is the lion, and Neil Conway is the fox. If it is a rematch that Conway wants, then it is a rematch that he will get.

AN UNEXPECTED VISITOR

There was not much else to be done in the way of investigation. Detective Smith had successfully cataloged the moves of all three of the convicts while the chief and Jefferson had done a small bout of profiling. For one of the first instances, Smith found himself waiting on the criminal to make the next move. In most cases, they were right behind their target, following them until the very end. But this time, they were right up with the culprit. Smith drove to his house with these thoughts on his mind. He stopped by the post office to see if his correspondent had reciprocated a letter. He had. The detective left the small building with a fresh envelope in his hand. He had recently taken up the pen to his valuable contact directly before the attempt on his life four months ago. Little did he know that this person was going to be one of the most important assets during his case. Not many people knew about his past, but if there were one person that he could always count on, it would be the person on the other end of the ink. Once he was back in the familiar surrounding of his office living room, he sat down to read the letter. Only four short lines were scribbled out on the small sheet of paper. Smith quickly took up a pen to write back. Midway through his second sentence he halted. He looked again at the small note.

Perhaps it is for the best. Also, if things become tense, it would do no harm for him to lend a helping hand.

Smith put his pen down, resolute in his decision to leave the current state of affairs alone. His phone's buzzing echoed on the wood of his desk. Expecting a call, he glanced down only to see that instead of a number, a battery life warning was glaring up at him. Only one bar remained in his power supply. He shrugged and disregarded it. It still had a ways to go until it was fully dead, anyways. The detective thought back to the thoughts and reasoning that the chief and his deputy gave on the three criminals' expertise. He fully trusted the powers of deduction of his two allies, so set out to expand on them himself. He picked up his pen once more and turned the note over so as to write out his findings. This process of his had become handy in the past, so why not try it again? Smith started out by relaying the information giving onto the sheet of paper. He wrote the three names of the criminals side by side.

Neil Conway. Saunders Macleod. Mystery Man

Next, he wrote the suspected roles that each one played. Under Conway, he wrote "experience with police, renowned con man." Under Macleod was "physique, ability to incapacitate guard." He came to the third convict and looked hard at the name.

What is missing in this list? What more is needed to enact the perfect escape plan? Experience and knowledge about the adversary is given. The means of escaping your incarceration also are provided.

All of a sudden, a single word popped into his mind.

Information. Information on the area would be needed because Conway does not know the surrounding area very well. Information on the cause of the escape, if Conway did not already know what that was, would be a must.

Feeling like he had hit upon the reason why the third man was involved, he scribbled out Information under the third convict's name. The fact that the name was still unknown bothered Smith slightly, but there was nothing he could do on that front. Detective Smith stood out from his office chair and decided that it was time that he did everything in his power to stop Conway from picking a new target before he actually did the deed.

The heat of the day had died down a small amount with the beginning of evening. Smith's clock read five on the dot. He had a good few hours of work ahead of him before he would consider wrapping up the day's work. The detective's new challenge was to get inside the mind of his adversary's thought process. That would be the only completely efficient way to correctly gauge which target his sights were on. Smith immediately discounted all the previous targets that had been hit by him. Almost all of those required time and massive amounts of planning, both of which Conway did not have. An art theft was also out of the question.

It is true that it would provide a good profit if he could sell it off speedily enough, but the fact that he has made himself known as an international taker of art would cause many galleries to be on high alert. He would be mistaken if he thought that art collectors overseas would soon forget the mark he made. Instead,

Smith turned his attention a little closer to home. He had a nagging feeling that Conway would attempt a fast and furious strike at a random time and place. Not to begin his second reign but to produce a sufficient enough smokescreen to cover his escape into a safer environment. This was what Smith was after. A target that would cause an uproar of activity, directed at the entirely wrong place. He drove through the center of downtown, physically looking at a place that would be most vulnerable. Smith shifted his mind to the one of a con man, so as to gain a different vantage point on things. He was struck by how many potential targets he found.

Businesses that were hiring new customers could easily be infiltrated and stolen from, countless citizens who could be fooled, and above all, even banks with faulty systems could be hacked. Assuming that Conway's aim would be a financial one, Smith scrutinized the targets with greater opportunities that would give him a quick buck. Unless Conway was planning to flat-out rob a storeowner, Smith could not see any opportunities for a fast con that would give the means by which one could use to escape. What Smith truly needed was a look into a criminal's mind—an encyclopedia of the way things are from the other side. The only problem was that Smith did not have the advantage of having a convicted felon on speed dial. But he did, however, happen to know of a jewelry store robber who was currently on his way through the procedure of being processed.

Detective Smith pulled up to the police HQ with a hopeful attitude. If fortune were on his side, then Steven Johnson, criminal grandeur, would be able to provide a rare eye into the world of crime. Mrs. Clark, the department's receptionist, knew the four-story building like the back of her hand. Smith approached Mrs. Clark.

"Hello, Detective, how may I help you today?" she offered with a friendly smile.

"Hello, Mrs. Clark. Do you happen to know if a man by the name of Steven Johnson is still going through the consequences of being caught?" Smith asked cordially.

"One moment, let my check my computer." It was not long before she returned.

"Mr. Johnson is in interrogation room B. All the interrogation rooms are located on the third floor," she answered before Smith had even asked. He thanked her and proceeded to the elevator. The interrogation rooms were lined up along both walls of the third floor. The processing station was located in the middle of the octagon-shaped room. Rooms A–H fanned clockwise starting from the northern tip of the pattern. Smith walked around the floor until the correct letter was in front of him. Room B was simple enough. A clear glass, one-sided mirror was positioned in a way that overlooked the small room with a single table and two chairs. To the detective's mild surprise, Jefferson was the interrogator. In Smith's opinion, there was not much interrogating going on. Steven Johnson looked more than willing to answer the deputy's inquiries. Detective Smith entered the area through a tiny door to his left.

"I wouldn't necessarily call them partners. More like acquaintances. Hey, Detective! What are you doin' here?" Johnson said excitedly. Jefferson turned to the doorway.

"Detective, here to join in on the interrogation?" Jefferson asked.

"Actually, Deputy Trueman, I am here to ask Mr. Johnson here a few questions. Would it inconvenience you if I stepped in a moment?"

"By all means, Detective." Jefferson motioned toward Johnson.

"I've got to say, Detective, I am mighty glad to see you!" Johnson said with a grin on his face.

"Thank you, Mr. Johnson. If the chief inspector has not already told you, you are being granted a public defender for your case," Smith said. This seemed to satisfy the man in front of him.

"Good enough for me! Whatcha want to ask me, Detective?"

"Were you at anytime associated with anyone who claimed to be a con man?"

"Well, Detective, in order to keep up my 'criminal grandeur' status I had to try my luck at being a con man." Smith had no idea that being a criminal grandeur required so much upkeep.

"How long have you practiced being a con man?"

"Oh, about a year. I wasn't very good at it though." Johnson sighed. Even though he probably was not the best person to be talking to for potential targets, Smith decided to continue the questioning.

"What kind of targets did you choose as your brief stunt as a con man?" Johnson thought for a minute.

"Mostly, people that looked like they could be fooled easily. I was never any good at the job, so I tried my luck at the quick and easy cons that got me some moolah. Ya know, the green stuff with the faces on it?" Johnson explained as if Smith was not savvy with different terms for money.

"If you were to acquire a target today, what would you pick as being the easiest to con?" Smith asked. This question was the possible smoking gun that he needed.

"Funny you should ask that, Detective. Just recently, I was lookin' for some easy money and asked that very same question. The only problem was that I couldn't find one! All of the ones that I found would have taken *way* too long to do. So instead, I went into the very jewelry store that I got caught for robbing. And so, we have made a full circle Detective," Johnson finished.

"Is there anything else you would like to ask, Detective?" Jefferson asked, striding over to Johnson and standing behind him.

"That will be all, Deputy Trueman. Thank you for letting me interrupt your process. Mr. Johnson, I wish you the best with your trial." Smith shook hands with Jefferson and then Johnson in turn. Detective Smith followed them out of room B.

"Bye, Detective! Good luck with your investigation!" Johnson called once they parted ways.

Despite being no closer to establishing a suitable target, Smith left the police department with a cheerful outlook. If he could not find what he was looking for, there was a more than likely chance that Conway would have an equally hard time doing so also. Although this was encouraging, Smith did not discount the possibility entirely. If Steven Johnson, an amateur criminal, could not find someone to con, it does not mean that Neil Conway, an experienced con man, would not. Smith became conscious that his hand was still on the handle of his car door. He had become so engrossed in his thoughts that he completely forgot about the world around him. He hopped in and started his car. Before he could put it in drive, a young officer came running to his window.

"Detective, the chief just informed me that he got a lead off the tip line. Apparently, someone saw one of the convicts. He asked me to tell you to meet him right away." She gave Smith the address and jogged back to the building she came from. Ecstatic to have a new lead to follow, the detective clicked his car into drive and sped off to the chief's location. The address that was given to Smith took him to a rather large farm in the middle of, very literally, nowhere. He wagered that there was not another living soul within twenty miles. The chief was conversing with a man that could not have looked more out of place. He was wearing a pitch-black suit with a dark-red tie, accompanied by dark shades to match. He gave an uninterested look when the detective pulled up.

"May want to ask a few questions of his own. In fact, here he is right now."

"Good evening, Chief. Is this the man who observed one of our convicts?" Smith asked politely.

"That would be my wife, actually. She was cleaning the kitchen when she saw a large man matching the description of one of the people who escaped from that prison. She watches the news every night and recognized who he was," the man wearing a suit said.

"Did your wife happen to see if anyone else was with this man?"

"Not that she saw. He was alone just trampling through our turnips. And I know what you are probably thinking. How could farmers look so nice and have a fairly decent home? Well, not all farmers are poor and uneducated." It seemed like this was not the first time that he gave this speech.

"I respect the hard work that you and your wife accomplish, sir," Smith responded. The chief pulled him over, away from the ears of the irritated farmer.

"Detective, I get a feeling that this man doesn't like law enforcement much. I suggest we wait until his wife gets back. Might be able to get more out of her," the chief said in a hushed tone.

"Just one more question, Chief. This is imperative." Smith turned back to face the witness's husband. "Did your wife ever refer to this man by his name?"

"Can't see what that has to do with anything, but yes. I believe that she called him Sledgehammer or something like that. Some nickname, no doubt." Detective Smith paused and stared hard at the man.

"I just have one more inquiry. How did your spouse know that the convict assumed the nickname Sledgehammer? I caught a glance of the news report and the nickname of Sledgehammer was nowhere to be found."

"Maybe she heard it in town. Why does it matter?"

"Sir, that nickname was given to him while he was in prison. The only conceivable way that your wife would have any knowledge regarding that name was if he or another one of his prison mates revealed it to her," Smith said slowly. The farmer took off his sunglasses to better look at his wife's accuser.

"Are you accusing my wife of talking to people who broke out of prison?" Smith needed to carefully word his next few responses. If he didn't, he might lose a substantial lead.

"No, sir, I am merely stating the facts. Have you had any visitors recently? Someone could have very well told your wife to notify the police that she witnessed one of the escapees walking through her garden."

"Now that you mention it, we did have a visitor. I was leaving for work when I saw a man with what appeared to be money in his hand. Do you think that he bribed my wife to call the tip line?" His tone had changed from anger to intrigue.

"It is very possible."

"If he told me to do it, I probably would have. He talked very smoothly. Made it really convincing." The chief shot a glance at Smith.

"Thank you for answering our questions."

The detective and the chief inspector walked slowly away from the farm.

"I can't believe it. Conway was here. What is he playing at, Detective?"

"Chief, he is toying with us. Attempting to gauge how we react. You know his process as well as I do. Assert your dominance and control over the situation and you have gone a great length to ensuring your victory. So far, it has been about a show of power. But once we catch on to even an iota of his trail, we will be right behind him every step of the way."

"But until then, what can we do? Every time we get a decent lead, it turns out to be a dead-end," the chief said, shaking his head sadly.

"Keep faith, Chief. There will always be something to follow. Every time you swing the axe, you cannot always strike gold. But the more you swing, the more likely you are going to go home with your treasure. This excursion has been more useful to us than you might think," Smith said with a kind smile.

"How do you figure?"

"We are a long way from the penitentiary, Chief," Smith prompted, hoping to get the chief to see the connection. Since this clue did not involve reconstructing events or detaching your mind from the present, he hit upon it with ease.

"Transportation! There's no way they walked all the way out here to the middle of nowhere."

"You just might have found your gold, Chief," Smith responded with a twinkle in his eye. The two of them examined the surrounding area, looking for any telltale signs of the escapees' mode of transportation. After a mile and a half of walking, they finally found their first real piece of evidence. Two distinct tire impressions were visible in the soft ground.

"I know these tracks. They are a certain brand of mountain bike. They're 29ers, if I'm not mistaken. Definitely 29ers. I picked up a couple of teenagers for stealing this same brand. I would know that tire track anywhere," the chief commented, bending down to get a better view.

"Impressive, Chief," Smith commended.

"I find it hard to believe that they came all this way on bicycles. When we get back to the station, I'll do a search of any of the bicycle venders in the area. With any luck, we might be able to see where they stole them from." It was the detective's turn to analyze the tracks. The two tracks were evenly spaced apart, giving the other enough room to turn. Both tracks slowly turned to the right, going more up hill as the turn became more pronounced. The impression of the turn was deeper than the first initial mark. Detective Smith stood up, confident with his findings.

"I can say with reasonable proof that the two men on bicycles set out in heading north." Smith pointed toward the right hand turn. The chief raised his eyebrows at the detective.

"How can you tell that?"

"The more the tracks go right, the deeper the impressions. To counter the forces of the turn, you must lean into it. The more pressure you put on the turn, the deeper the impressions. Say they were turning the opposite direction. The tracks would remain the same. But we are saved by the uphill slant. If they were headed down the hill, both marks would have the same impression depth. But since the track that is going uphill is deeper, we can conclude that they were heading in that general direction." The chief nodded his assent. He was becoming more used to the detective's analytical powers.

"Should we follow them? If Conway knew that we were going to come here, he would probably figure on us following the tracks," the chief said.

"I agree with you there, Chief. He most likely would count on us trailing them. But we have to consider the situation. We know that they did in fact travel in that direction. Until we have seen tracks going in the other direction to disprove it, it will remain our working hypothesis."

"I think that we should find ourselves a handy map of the area. I'm not really in the mood for walking in the middle of nowhere for hours on end," the chief grumbled. Smith agreed and they set off to find a map. The only map, unfortunately, was in a tourist town back in the direction that they came. The sun was beginning to make its descent in the sky, so the idea to study the map in the police department was unanimous. As they gazed at the map, they were pleasantly surprised to see that the farm that they had just come from was charted. This gave them an excellent heading from which to start the trail. Starting a little to the east of the farmhouse, they followed the direction of the tire impressions. About ten miles from the beginning of the tracks was another small farm. Next to the name was a small *V*, signaling that the land was vacant.

"Chief, we just might have found the end to our tracks," Smith postulated.

"I'm not taking chances on this one, Detective. Jefferson!" the chief bellowed down the hall. Hurried footsteps could be heard coming down the hall. Their owner quickly appeared in sight.

"You called, boss?"

"We are going to this small farmhouse. There is a more than likely chance that our perps either passed through there or are there now."

"Do you want me to alert the gang?"

"Keep this between you and me for now. Don't want to stir anybody up. You want to come along, Detective?"

"No, thank you, Chief. I have had enough adventure to last me one day," Smith answered.

"Suit yourself. Come on, Jefferson!" The chief snatched his keys from the hook and charged off with Jefferson following behind. Detective Smith concluded that he had accomplished a good day's work. He would get a fresh start early tomorrow. After opening the entrance doors, he was struck by how dark it had become. The wind had picked up to a decent-enough speed to cause stumbling if one was not careful. Smith drove carefully to his modest house through the windy night. His thoughts bundled up all of the clues that had been accumulated throughout the day. Smith was struck with the thought that there was something oddly familiar about the third convict. He quickly filed it away for future thought. His footsteps on the walkway to his door were overpowered by the noise of the wind. A strange, eerie feeling had gripped him as he put his key in the keyhole of his front door. He inspected the lock and found that there were scratches all around the keyhole. Smith was absolutely certain they had not been there before. His brain immediately recalled the circumstances surrounding the last break-in. It had not been a pleasant experience. Smith then stooped to the ground. Clearly visible was one distinct boot print. Detective Smith pushed open his door and prepared to meet his intruder. The only thing that met him was the darkness of his entry hall. Smith did not dare drop his guard as he approached his door and slowly walked through the threshold. Every sense was on high alert. As he went to turn on the light, a calculated voice spoke through the darkness.

"Detective Smith. It's been a while." The intruder clicked a lamp, illuminating his face. Detective Smith locked eyes with his old assistant, Riley Stevens. His former right-hand man was the third convict, and he was pointing the barrel of a handgun directly at him.

A KINK IN THE PLAN

Intense silence was shared between the two former colleagues: one, a renowned detective and the other, an escapee from prison who was about to enact his revenge upon the one person who put him there. Detective Smith looked into the hardened eyes of his former assistant. Incarceration had done much to change his appearance. His face was gaunter and had a rough look to it, an attribute that he had not had when Smith knew him last. The constant workout had made him assume a more intimidating aspect. Finally, one of the men spoke.

"Four months I was stuck in that prison. For weeks, I thought about my revenge and how to act upon it. I had a vague idea of how to do so, when I was lucky enough to stumble across Neil Conway. I remember Conway well, Detective. He filled me in on any parts that I was missing. He told me all about the little duel that you both had. I can't say that I'm not a little impressed. But once he took me into his group and told me his plan, I knew what I had to do. I was assigned with one major task after our escape plan was successful: to find and eliminate the threat against us. Conway knew that with you out of the equation, everything would be smooth sailing." Detective Smith had not uttered a sound during his former assistant's monologue. His mind was quickly working a way out of his current scenario. From his perspective, there was nothing that could be done to alter the situation. He was entirely at the mercy of the man in front of him. "I came here for only one thing." Riley Stevens slowly walked and positioned himself at arms length from the detective. "To ask for your forgiveness." Smith thought he had misunderstood until he looked down and saw that his former assistant had extended his gun free hand. Detective Smith slowly shook hands with his would-be assassin.

"If you did not come to my house with the intention to kill, then why are you here?" Smith asked gingerly.

"To warn you, Detective." With relief, Smith could tell that the tough-guy routine had been dropped. The Riley Stevens that Smith knew had returned.

"To warn me that one of the most dangerous men that I have ever come into contact is trying to take me out of the picture?"

Riley smiled at the detective's words. "I knew that you hadn't lost your touch. Not after you handled Conway's previous attempt," Riley said.

"Enlighten me, Riley. If you were not positioned in Conway's group, plotting your revenge, then what exactly were the conditions?" Smith questioned. Riley gestured to a chair. Smith sat down in the armchair directly across from Riley.

"I guess I should start at the beginning. After you caught me and put me in jail, I was angry, to say the least. In fact, I did try and figure out a way to get back at you. But after a while, I sincerely regretted what I had done. I had potentially destroyed the respect of one of my best friends. Not to mention my partner in catching crime. By the time that I caught the attention of Conway, I was dedicated to living out the rest of my sentence and then devoting myself to repairing what I had done. This plan was altered with Neil Conway. He came to me wanting information mainly about you and the police department. I was christened with the nickname of Informant because of the knowledge I possessed. I eventually figured out their plan to escape and come after you, so I volunteered to be the one to do it. I wanted a chance to warn you about the threat. When Conway tried to send a hit man after you, I warned him that it wouldn't get him anywhere. Well, I was right.

"This increased my reputation in the group. Slowly, I built up trust with the two men. After escaping, I tracked you down. I was right in assuming that you had moved houses. I had to tread carefully though. I knew that you would be on to me and that I wouldn't have a lot of time once you started. Believe me, I have seen too many criminals go down because of your efforts. To say the least, I was shaking in my boots. I had to risk calling you in order to track you. This led me to your house. The rest, you know. As to the gun, I ran out of space in my backpack," Riley concluded. He now looked at the detective apologetically. Detective Smith analyzed what he had said. There was nothing to be gained out of him coming here to lie. If he were, he would have already completed his end of the so-called deal. It did not take Smith long to conclude his thoughts.

"The fact that you would go to that great of length to ensure my safety is a testament to your request for forgiveness. In short, I forgive you." At the detective's words, Riley sighed, as if a great weight had been lifted off of his shoulders.

"Thank you, Detective," he said, mustering up all the meaning he could. With the pleasantries aside, it was now time to get down to business. A treasure trove of information and leads had fallen directly into Smith's lap. He would be very amiss not to take it.

"Riley, what exactly do you know of Conway's plans?" he seriously inquired.

"Not much. What I told you is about the extent of what I know. He didn't tell his exact plans to anyone. I do, however, happen to know the assigned meeting place. It is a small farmhouse practically in the middle of nowhere." Smith was positive that it was the farmhouse that the chief and Jefferson were not in the process of checking.

"No need to worry about that aspect. The chief inspector and his deputy are searching it as we speak," Smith assured. Riley's face fell at the mention of the chief. Even the detective could not fully ascertain the chief's reaction to the news that Riley was out and about.

"You probably know more information about what is going on than I do. But I doubt that you will find Conway there. He mentioned to us that staying in a single place for too long was not part of his plan," Riley conveyed.

"We can only hope for the best," Smith replied.

"Be careful, Detective. Conway wants another face-off. We both know what he is capable off."

"Do not fret about that. I will do everything in my power to stop him from escaping. This game is far from over." Detective Smith meant every word that he said. Now that he had an inside man, things were looking a little more promising. Smith was certain that Conway was not expecting this kink in his plan. "The only thing left to guarantee is the safety of yourself. There is no insight into the mind of Neil Conway. He will find out that he lost one of his assets. We need to make sure that he cannot act upon his feelings."

"And how are we going to do that?" It was evident that Riley had not thought about the possible consequences of his actions.

"We are going to have to involve the chief. It is the only foolproof way to make certain that you receive protection."

"But… Whatever you think is best, Detective," he responded reluctantly. The wind continued to howl outside in the night environment. Riley had not done much to add additional information, but he had proved the certainty of Smith's deductions. A knock on Smith's door fought to be heard over the wind. It had died down a good amount since Smith arrived home. Riley looked around, presumably trying to find a place to hide. The detective motioned for Riley to stay still and opened the door. It was the chief inspector.

"Detective, I tried calling you, but this blasted gust of wind knocked out service. Luckily, it is supposed to have stopped by morning," he explained. The chief took four steps into the house and then noticed the man trying to blend into the chair.

"Hey, Chief. Long time no see," he said shyly. A look of outrage and confusion was clearly visible on the chief's face. He pulled his firearm and aimed it at Riley.

"Riley Stevens? Aren't you supposed to be in jail?" Then it dawned on him. "You're the third convict? Decided on a little nighttime visit to the detective's place, didn't you?" he shot at Riley. Riley attempted to explain the situation, but it did nothing to ease the chief's energy.

"Chief, it is all right. Mr. Stevens just concluded his very engaging narrative. If you give him a moment, everything will be clear," Smith said calmly. The chief lowered his weapon.

"I trust your judgment, Detective." Riley once again launched into his story. By the end of it, the chief still looked suspicious but had dropped the anger. "Sounds a little fishy, but I didn't become the chief inspector without being able to tell when someone is lying. And from what I can tell, you aren't lying." Riley Stevens fell back on to the chair exhaustedly.

"Thank you, Chief. What is it that you came here to tell me? Luck with the farmhouse, I hope?" Smith asked.

The chief glanced at Riley then began. "Unfortunately, Detective, we can't do anything until these winds die down. And I doubt that, if they are there, Conway won't be doing much traveling either."

"I agree completely." After their conversation died down, Riley stood up uneasily.

"Uh, Chief? I know that I am not the person that you want to be hearing from right now, but the detective had the thought that Conway might come after me. Is there anything that you can do to help me?" Riley asked carefully.

"I'm still not sure about you, Stevens, but I'm not heartless. I will see what I can do to give you protection. But don't forget that the law must be upheld. After this thing is through, you will have to go through the consequences of your actions," the chief said.

"Don't worry, Chief. I will do whatever is needed."

"Good. You are going to have to come with me. No sense in waiting to get you protection. Detective, I will see you tomorrow for the search of that farmhouse." The chief shook the detective's hand and motioned for Riley to follow him. The two of them left Smith's house and made their way to the police HQ.

Once he was alone, Smith sat down in his familiar office chair to analyze the current swing the case had suddenly taken. The information brought to him by his former assistant was too valuable to discount but at the same time slightly suspicious. He knew Conway's methods too well, and somehow, he doubted that the infamous con man would make such a grave mistake. The problem was, however, the close proximity that the tracks had to the exact location given by Riley. It was no coincidence. Contradictions and speculations flew around Smith's head as he determined to find the correct path amongst many dead-ends. Detective Smith stood up with his mind settled. He quickly procured the darkest clothing he could find and threw open his door to the sound of howling wind. Thus, Detective Smith's night investigation had begun.

Neil Conway knew too much about the procedures of this case to be caught off guard by an investigation in the morning. He expected the police to be predictable. It was for this reason that Detective Smith, under the guise of night, carried out an action that would be considered suicidal by normal standards. The detective needed to be unpredictable, and rushing into a likely hideout of two escaped convicts was just the action to become so. The field that housed the small building was much more imposing at night. Without the light of the sun to guide him, Smith had to call upon his memory of the geography of the area from the map that he and the chief had gazed over. His vigil was long and tedious, and after an hour or so, he started to wonder if his mind had failed him. Smith's unease was settled by the appearance of a small silhouette on the horizon. Within minutes, he was bracing himself from the wind on the northern side of the farmhouse. Smith strained his ears for any sound that might be audible over the monstrous roaring of the gale, but none could be heard.

Suddenly, a strange feeling that he should act enveloped the detective. This new wave of instinct heightened his senses, enabling him to pick out a tiny screeching noise emanating from within the house. Smith instantly recognized the sound of wood scraping across wood and knew that his targets were making a break for the window on the opposite side of the house. Without pausing to think, Detective Smith broke down the front door with his shoulder and was just in time to see a figure easily slip himself through the window. The detective knew that his adversary was too lean and nimble to give chase to, especially in this weather. Instead of running aimlessly into the night, Smith took advantage of his situation and looked over the small building with his expertly trained eye. The room in which he stood was plain and simple. Partially rotten wood covered the floor while four sheets of plywood made up the walls. The only furniture visible was a small table with two chairs. One of the chairs was pushed back hastily. Smith identified this as the chair in which Conway was sitting before being interrupted. The other chair caught his attention and yielded an interesting fact. The con man was alone in the farmhouse. It was not what was there, but what wasn't there that called this clue into light. Aside from the one chair, everything else was in its place. No other furniture showed signs of strain from having anybody on them, especially not a massive Scot. On the tiny table stood a lone map, with different locations in the surrounding areas circled in a dark red.

Conway was already preparing to move hideouts. It appears I was correct in my assumption.

Detective Smith spent a few more minutes going over the rest of the farmhouse, but found nothing else of interest. On his way out, he pocketed the small map, resolving to show it to the chief first thing in the morning.

Morning arrived speedily for the detective. Granted that he had spent the majority of his night hunting down convicts, it still surprised him. Lack of sleep had very little effect on Smith. He had long since been accustomed to long nights and early days because of his cases. Therefore, it was no shock to Smith that the receptionist gave him a funny look when he stated that he wished to converse with the chief at this early hour. The chief's countenance was one of tiredness as he darted his eyes up from his paperwork when Smith entered.

"Good morning, Chief! I take it that you spent a sleepless night also?" The chief leaned back in his chair and sighed.

"Spot on, Detective. I spent all of my night trying to get Stevens into official protection. It normally would be no problem, but the mayor was more than a little strict on letting a convict into the system. I'm still not sure if his story isn't one big hoax, but I pushed for protection anyway. Did you figure out anything that could make this whole investigation clearer?" the chief asked, shaking himself out of his frustration at the mayor.

"Actually, Chief, I am here about the possible safe house that our escapees might be utilizing."

"You mean the farmhouse? I hate to tell you this, Detective, but I still need to finish this paperwork until Stevens is safe. Let me call up Jefferson to go with you. He's been itching to get back out in the field." Before the chief could dial up Jefferson, Smith intervened.

"That will not be necessary, Chief, although I might require Officer Trueman for the next process of my investigation. I took the liberty of conducting an investigation of the farmhouse late last night. Conway knows our procedures inside and out, Chief. By acting during a span of time that he did not expect, I very nearly had him in my grasp. He escaped through a window, but not before leaving behind a map of locations that he was studying," Smith said with confidence and assurance. Instead of being angered at the detective's actions, the chief was ecstatic.

"Detective, you don't know how glad I am that you are on this case. Was there anything on this map that could help us?" Smith pulled out the folded up map and tossed it onto the chief's desk. He quickly unfolded it and furrowed his eyebrows when he saw it. "There are a lot of places here, Detective. Should we search them all?"

"It might just be profitable to do so. Saunders Macleod, the Scotsman, was not present in the farmhouse when I entered. It is safe to assume that he could very well be at one of these alternate locations. Conway knows that we have the map. He very well could use that as a feint to attract our attention away from the real location of his accomplice," Smith explained. The chief contemplated this flow of speculation.

"Hold on. If Conway saw you, then he has to know that Stevens failed in his assassination of you, Detective. If he tries to go after Stevens, we have him."

"I would not use the resources, Chief. Conway is intent upon escaping from us. I doubt that he would walk straight into an obvious trap."

"Then if we can't get Conway, let's take down Macleod," the chief remarked with energy.

"Exactly what I was going to say myself. Without Conway, Macleod will have lost the mastermind behind their plans. We need to exploit this as soon as possible."

The chief's eyes fell on the map once again, and an idea was visible in his mind.

"Detective, we know that the two of them made it to the farmhouse because of the tire tracks. Maybe Macleod was supposed to go find another place to stay. What if Conway expected us to burst in at any moment and was eager to find another safe house?" the chief quickly announced. Smith thought about the possibility of such a claim and nodded his approval.

"Excellent idea, Chief! I recommend checking the nearby settlements and inquiring if any inhabitant has seen a very large Scot."

"I'm on it, Detective! We might just nail these degenerates yet!" the chief said, as he grabbed his desk phone and started calling various departments. Until the cavalry arrived, there was not much for Detective Smith to undertake. If they succeeded in their search, a major blow will have been dealt to Conway's plans. Without someone to help him get away cleanly, it will only be a matter of time before he is once again apprehended. Detective Smith's thoughts landed on his correspondent. If all went well, the need for him here would be extinguished. Smith decided to let the cards fall where they may and not discourage his writer from traveling. As he left the chief to his duties, Smith could not help but feel a little uneasy. Every time that he and the police thought they were close to catching one of the bad guys it turned out that they were even farther away than previously thought. Why would this instance be any different? Detective Smith decided to employ his ultimate weapon: He would place himself in

Conway's shoes and go over every inch of this case with a fine-toothed comb. Smith chose the best location to engage his mind in his thoughts. He settled himself into his comfy office chair and began the art of deduction for which his profession relies upon. Smith started with the breakout. He would have done the same thing in Conway's shoes.

Apply the strengths of your comrades in your plan to ensure that you have the best possible outcome. After both guards are incapacitated, find the nearest cover, a.k.a, the forest. Once in the forest, send one of your men who knows the most about the target to find and eliminate said target while the rest find a place to settle down. Next, plant a seed for the police to follow while staying perfectly hidden under the cover of ignorance. If too much time passes before I hear from my outside man, I would establish a new place to hide while I wait out the delay. I would not hide out in any of the nearby towns, since the arrival of two strangers who matched the descriptions of the convicts would surely alert the citizens. Thus, I send my other man out to find a place while I determine the next move of the police. With not a minute to spare, I realize that my position is blown and proceed to escape. No contact between the rest of the men is possible, so what do I do? Take advantage of the police's follies and exploit them. Only once has the police department made a mistake…The three houses that were futilely searched and now presumed useless.

Detective Smith was silent, both mentally and physically. This game between Conway and himself was starting to seem more like a duel. Blow after blow is given, but neither of them is closer or farther away from their goal as the next. Conway and Detective Smith are essentially the same person, just with different motives and uses of the gift that was given to them. Detective Smith could not resist the thought that Conway would never be caught but would never truly escape. Smith smiled without merriment at the idea that he was chasing himself, just in a different form. He could almost guarantee that the con man felt the same feeling. The detective may never capture Conway, but he at least could ensure that no more innocent people suffered under his evil talent. Before he quit the chief's office, he told him that should he get the call to battle while Smith was occupied, to go ahead and conduct the search. He postulated that the chief would be on his way, with the police department behind him, to search all of the small settlements in the area. Smith tried to call the chief, but found that his phone had died during the night. He would have to face whoever was on the other side of that safe house alone. Detective Smith resolved himself in his actions and set out to usher in the beginning of the end to his case.

END GAME

The snarl of the winds had died down with the morning and a peaceful, calm day had taken its place. A few billowy clouds had risen in the horizon but were too white to threaten rain. The calmness was almost enough to force Detective Smith to stop his car on the side of the road and just enjoy the day. If it was not for his current case, he certainly would have been tempted. While he was driving, he observed several police cars speed by him at well over the speed limit. Smith knew that this was a signal that the chief's search had already begun. His search, however, was concentrated on populated areas, while Smith's was three lonely buildings in the middle of nowhere. Since this was the third time that Smith had been in this area, he had at his disposal a detailed map of the region. The three houses rose up from the horizon with alarming pace. Aside from the three shadows of the structures, the prairie was deserted of objects. That is, until a rather large lump emerged from one of the edifices and made its way slowly across the field.

Detective Smith immediately knew that this was his man. He was on a small dirt road that connected the main town to one of the smaller settlements a few miles eastward. Smith shut off his car and attempted to make himself appear as though he were a lonely tree on the field. He tracked the Scotsman's progress for a few minutes, not daring to move until he knew it was safe. His target disappeared behind a large oak tree. Presently, Smith heard the low rumble of a motorcycle's engine. The machine shot from its hiding place and set off toward the detective's hiding place. Fearing detection, he ducked down behind the wheel to give the impression that an empty car had broken down on the side of the road. The illusion worked, and the Scot drove onward.

Smith brought his vehicle to life and tailed the motorcycle at an appropriate distance. Once ten minutes had elapsed, the large man finally turned down the dirt road and on to the more common streets of the city. Bewilderment spread through Smith as he drove even deeper into the city. He could have never guessed that the convict's hidden abode was so close to home. In this case, the old axiom of hiding in plain sight seemed to suffice. The detective was still unsure on how he was to apprehend a man who was at least twice his size without sustaining some hideous injury. He put these thoughts aside, however, when the motorcycle pulled into the parking lot of a small, rundown motel and the man hopped off. Smith parked his car two blocks down from the motel and jogged up to the front door of the inn. He noticed that the motorcycle had no license plate, a fact that he stored for later. Theft, in addition to escaping jail, probably won't look too good to a jury. As the detective casually waltzed into the inn, he took a quick inventory of the people that were sitting at the small tables scattered about. There was only one man present, and he appeared to be sleeping with his hat covering his eyes and face. The stranger was in a far corner, so Smith decided not to worry about him interfering. Turning to the front desk, he observed that the owner of this hotel, if it can be called that, was not at his post. *All the better*, Smith thought to himself as he climbed the stairs. The thunderous footsteps of his target could be heard hitting the ceiling above his head. He crested the final stair in time to see which door Macleod entered. Detective Smith walked quickly to the door and knocked on the wood.

"Who's ther'?" the strong Scottish accent responded.

"Detective Smith, but I am assured that you already know that, Mr. Macleod." The door suddenly flew open and the mountain of a man was before the detective. He was not as tall as Smith but had enough muscle to compensate for his lack of height. Shock and awe filled the man's features as he beheld the man who was supposed to be dead. It took a few seconds for the Scot to realize why the detective was here. Once he did, he seized Smith by the shoulders and hurled him down the hall. Detective Smith nimbly landed on his feet and gave chase to the man who was fleeing down the stairs. By the time the detective hit the ground floor, Macleod was already throwing open the door leading to freedom. Before he could get out of the motel, a strange thing happened. The stranger, who was now very much awake, put a hand on the Scot's shoulder, and pulled him to the ground. The man on the ground made a mad reach for a fire stoker. The stranger was quicker and pointed the weapon at Macleod.

"No, you don't, laddie." The stranger's hat had fallen off in the scuffle, exposing his face. Detective Smith walked over and extended a hand to his brother. The two siblings shook hands. "I take it that you got my letters, then?"

"Indeed, I did. How did you find me?" Smith asked. His brother looked down at the flabbergasted Scot, and then back up at Smith.

"I like to believe that you are not the only one with whom the powers of deduction have been given. So this is the accomplice that Conway used to escape?"

"Mr. Macleod supplied the physical aspect to the getaway, incapacitating one of the guards on duty with a well thrown boulder," Smith told his brother. "I see that you have been by my house. Did you perhaps notice anything involving the chief inspector?"

"In fact, I did. There was a young deputy at your door who was looking for you. I gave him the address of this motel and told him to bring his boss. They should be here shortly," Smith's brother said.

"Thank you. Your help has been invaluable. Without you, it is very probable that I would have ended where I had started."

"You would have figured it out. I was just here to lend a brief helping hand in catching this man. I am heading back soon, though, and I wanted a chance to tell you to be careful in regards to Conway. You know, as well as I do how dangerous he can be. I best be off, or else questions might be asked as to why you have never mentioned me before. That certainly is a path that we do not want to take. I would rather that your past remain hidden," Smith's brother cautioned. Police sirens echoed in the distance, and Smith could make out the distinct tone of the chief's personal cruiser. His sibling heard it also, and with one last shake of the hand, he vanished out of the back door. An instant later, the chief and Jefferson burst in through the front door. When Jefferson saw that his hero had the convict apprehended, he put one fist in the air in victory.

"You got him, Detective!" The chief hauled Macleod to his feet and clasped handcuffs on him.

"I don't know how you do it, Detective. Not even escaped convicts are safe from the likes of you," the chief said.

"Us, Chief. Us. The amount of information that you and Officer Trueman bring in from the field is what truly aids me in my cases. I thank you for that," Detective Smith said. The three of them plus the Scot left the motel and headed back toward the police department. Once there, the chief handed off Saunders Macleod to be processed while he, the detective, and Jefferson went into his office.

"Well, Detective, another job well done. Two of the three escaped criminals are accounted for," the chief said.

"Chief, did you find anything of importance during your search?" Smith asked.

"At first, it seemed like a waste of time. I was starting to wonder whether or not I had made the right choice when we struck gold. One of the citizens in some tiny town came forward and told of a man who had come knocking at her door. He asked for help and then fainted. She took him into her house and went out to get a doctor. When she came back, all the money in her house was gone, along with her husband's clothes and car," the chief explained.

"It seems that our con man is at it again," Jefferson nodded.

"But now he has means of transportation and enough money to last him a while," the chief added. Detective Smith looked from the chief to Jefferson.

"We will get him, Chief. Do not worry. He may escape us this time, but he cannot elude us forever."

"Detective, do you think that there's still a chance we can get him?" Jefferson inquired of his idol.

"It appears as if he is making his exit. We got close to capturing him this time, and he knows it. Both of his most trusted men soon were in our grasp. Now that he has the means to escape, I believe that he will do so. Chief, this is our last opportunity to catch Neil Conway until he melts back into the shadows."

"What is our next step, Detective?" the chief asked with finality.

"Most likely, he will proceed to a form of transportation that is faster and more efficient than the one he employs presently."

"What about a train?" Jefferson asked.

"Precisely. Well done, Officer Trueman. Travel by train is the most probable. Conway will most likely procure passage while the train is in transit between two stations. This will guarantee that no one notices his entry, while making certain that he is unknown to everyone on board."

"Jefferson, go with the detective to the train station nearest to that small town that we got the report in.

Maybe we can at least make him change trains if we can lock that one down," the chief ordered.

"Aye aye, boss." Jefferson saluted and followed the detective out of the chief's office.

"Officer Trueman, you have the most knowledge of the landscape. You mind driving?" Smith tossed his keys to Jefferson, who looked as if he had just won a million dollars. He dropped the keys, but soon recovered them with a mumble of apology. Jefferson and Smith got in the car and were off. Now that they had some time to talk, the deputy decided to question the detective.

"In all actuality, Detective, what do you think are the odds of Conway going to this train?"

"Neil Conway is a smart and cunning man. He most likely has a fairly accurate idea of our next move. A benefit to us, however, is that we caught his co-conspirator . Possibly it made him anxious. Odds are a slippery slope with this man. You have to make his game your game. Change the rules to better suit you, and then, perhaps, a light may indeed shine at the end of the tunnel." Silence followed Detective Smith's monologue while the two men thought.

"Why exactly are you so determined to catch Conway? It seems like this is more to you than another criminal," Jefferson asked. Smith smiled a knowing smile.

"All the good qualities of the defenders of justice I see in him. The only difference lies in how one uses those talents. He for evil. You, the chief, and I for justice. Conway destroyed innocent lifestyles with his corruption, yet one cannot help but be awed at the way in which he does so. Take a masterful painting of a beautiful day. It inspires and promotes confidence and comfort. Now take that same painting and artist, but convert the day into night. All the fears and terrors of night are represented in this painting, yet it is still oddly beautiful. This is why he must be stopped. Motives mean little to Neil Conway. The fight between us and him is all that truly matters to him," Smith finished his explanation of his nemesis while Jefferson looked on with awe and fear.

"Detective, we will get him. It might have been hard then, but this is now. The chief and me will stop at nothing to apprehend this man. You can count on us." As the two men conversed, Jefferson had pulled Smith's car into the train station. The usual hustle-bustle of a main area of commerce greeted them as they stepped onto the platform. Nobody seemed the slightest bit disturbed that a convicted criminal could be walking in their midst. Detective Smith found the conductor of the vessel and pulled him to the side.

"Excuse me, sir. My name is Detective Smith, and I have reason to believe that a very dangerous man might be on your train presently." The conductor laughed.

"Heh, a dangerous man eh? Oh alright, you can search the compartments." After thanking the man, Smith motioned for Jefferson to come over and assist him in the search of the locomotive. The inside was packed with travelers, some from the current stop and others from the past station. Nowhere Smith looked did he see a con man in hiding. Jefferson shrugged the same result from his end of the train. The conductor soon came along and told the duo that their search was finished. As they stepped off the train, the whistle blew and the metal wheels screeched. Before long, Smith and Jefferson were the only two visible on the platform.

After the train had gone, Jefferson called up the chief to give him the news.

"It's a no go, Chief. No sign of Conway. Really? All right, I'll tell him. Adios, boss." Jefferson snapped his phone shut and walked over to where the detective was. "No luck on the other stations, Detective. Wherever Conway is, he certainly isn't near any trains."

"Thank you, Deputy Trueman. We still have one more card to play before I will condone a fold. Call the chief. Tell him to bring Saunders Macleod from interrogation and into his office, if he would be so kind," Smith asked. The drive back to the HQ went by fast. He had only once before been in the position of the interrogator, and the outcome of that occurrence led to his current case. When the detective and Jefferson entered the chief's office, they realized that most of the room was already taken up by a very large man.

"I did as you asked, Detective. Here is one Saunders Macleod," the chief presented.

"Thank you, Chief. Now, Mr. Macleod, I have a few questions about your employer, Mr. Neil Conway." The large man leaned forward on his knees and looked Smith in the eye.

"What do ya wan' to know?"

"Did your co-conspirator ever make mention of what he was going to do once he escaped the police?"

"He mentioned on' or two little jobs. Mostly, he said he was goin' to lay low for a wee bit," Macleod said casually. This news interested the detective. If that were true, then there was no sense in worrying about a threat far into the future.

"Why exactly did you three escape?"

"Conway needed a few men to launch his escape. He recruited me for me strength, and the o'er one, I believe he called him Informant, for his knowledge on you and the police. Conway wan'ed to get out and so did I." Smith glanced at the other two men in the room. By the way they had their eyes glued on the two of them, it was obvious that they did not want to interrupt.

"I just have one last inquiry, Mr. Macleod. How were you three going to escape the city, granted that you did not get caught?" The Scot thought for a moment before answering.

"We never knew. Conway kept the last bit of his plan to 'imself. Said he would tell when he was ready." Detective Smith stared at the ground at the conclusion of the Scot's statement. There was no reason to suspect a lie, but Smith secretly hoped it was so.

"Thank you for your time, Mr. Macleod." The chief signaled for one of his officers to take him away.

"If what he says is true, we may never find Conway," Jefferson said once the large man had left. Detective Smith considered the deputy's words. Every lead had been broken; no clue left unearthed. No breadcrumb was left to follow. The light that Smith had seen at the end of the tunnel was extinguished. Neil Conway had escaped.

"Chief, Mr. Trueman, I fear that we may have to let Neil Conway have this victory, at least until we have a suitable lead to follow. We will catch him, just not today. Mr. Macleod alluded to the fact that Conway is not going to step out onto the open for a period of time. I trust that we are free from him for the time being." The two other men nodded at Smith's words.

"Detective, I'll have to trust you on this one. But if he comes into my town again, you better believe that I will not stop until he has two new metal bracelets," the chief announced with vigor and pride.

"He can't get away from us twice," Jefferson concurred. Detective Smith produced an encouraging smile.

"In the meantime, we can busy ourselves with the curious problem or two that happens to come our way. Once again, I thank you for all of your assistance." Smith shook the hands of his two partners and walked, with a lighter step, out of the HQ. On his way toward his home, Smith's mind could not help but scrutinize the past few days. The feeling coursing through his veins was, surprisingly, one of completion. Aside from being assaulted with foolishness and disappointment, he happened to be marginally excited at discovering an intellectual match. The day will come, when the wits of both will be put to the final test, and one will emerge victorious. But until then, Smith would be perfectly content with analyzing any of the conundrums that stumbled into his residence.

The detective's thoughts searched for a topic, and somehow landed upon his brother. He had made the decision to hide his brother's involvement due to the fact that his sibling rarely enjoyed public attention and only appeared at a crucial moment. Whenever Smith required advice or assistance, he could always count upon his brother's letters to steer him on the correct path. No one else in the world knew every detail of the humble detective's complicated past. Thankfully, none asked questions regarding this aspect of his life, and this made his professional life easier. Not even the chief or Jefferson had an understanding about this. Detective Smith found himself at his front door once he snapped back into the correct time period. He tossed his 1890's style hat on the hook, hung up his very lengthy coat and proceeded into the kitchen area. Smith decided to cook up a quick homemade pizza for dinner. He had always had a knack for expertly constructing the perfect Italian meal. After throwing some sauce, cheese, and pepperonis onto the homemade dough, he stuck it in the oven. Smith slowly meandered over to his homey office area that doubled as his living room. A crisp, bright envelope that was precariously placed on the edge of the wood arrested his attention. The front read "Detective Smith" in a precise and delicate hand. This particular writing was oddly familiar to the detective. As he grasped the envelope, he was surprised to feel the heaviness of the contents within. Smith quickly ripped it open and read the few pages that tumbled out.

Detective Smith,

I must say that I really enjoyed our duel over the past few days. Your skills have increased expo-

nentially since the last time we met. You were very quick to figure out my true plan, Detective. In fact, I almost didn't get away. Getting this letter to you was difficult, to say the least. It set my plans back a few hours, but it had to be done. While it's on my mind, if you ever happen to run across the woman whose possession I stole—excuse me, borrowed—would you tell her that I apologize? I needed a mode of transportation, and she had one. It is true that I could have conned anyone, but I actually enjoyed the hospitality. My company over the past few months has been sketchy at best. Your old assistant, Riley Stevens, has a very promising future. I could easily recognize the touch of my most formidable opponent in the way that he analyzed a threat. Mr. Saunders Macleod was really only useful for his physique. It was no wonder that he was the first one to get caught. Just so you do not become confused, I am not counting your old right-hand man coming back as one of my men "getting caught." I had good reason to believe that he would not hurt you in any way. That is the main reason why I sent him instead of Macleod, or Sledgehammer, as the prison folk say. He was vital to my plan. I expected him to give up the location of our safe house, but what I did not expect was the time in which you struck.

I was counting on you and the chief inspector, a decent enough fellow, to storm the castle in the morning. You can imagine my surprise when I glimpsed your silhouette out of one of the windows. I was grateful that I had some expertise in yoga. Slipping out of a window is not as easy as it looks. Before you interrupted me and my map-gazing, I had sent the Scottish mountain to go and hunt for another safe house. This of course was just a ruse to warrant your attention. You latched on to my plan exactly as I hoped. Your chief inspector, however, landed closer to my true position. He raided the house that I stayed at only moments after I had taken off.

Now I come to the part of my story that was the most intriguing. I take it that you dialed up the chief after you had captured Macleod, and that shortly after, he told you of my exploits in that *small town. I wonder whose decision was it to search the train stations? Whosever, it was a smart move. I was worried that the coop had been flown when you walked up to me in the train station. I am glad to see that my disguise as the locomotive conductor was efficient enough to fool you.*

Don't beat yourself up for overlooking me. I would have done the same thing. A funny fact, some of the passengers actually came up to me and asked questions such as "What is the next stop? What time does the train leave? Where are some snacks?" Luckily, I knew enough about my escape plan to have knowledge on these things. I will go ahead and assure you that I am nowhere near your current location. No sense in troubling yourself to try and find me when I am far away, Detective. I know that a few little problems are present in your area, and you would do well to occupy yourself with those. Have no fear, Detective, I will reappear when the time is ripe and the moment is good. When I think about you and I, the Latin phrase "speculum imaginem" comes to mind. We are like mirror images of one another. I am sure that you have thought about this fact, and whether you agree or not, this phrase remains the truth.

If you wish to send this letter on to the chief, you may do so. It might even calm him down enough to concentrate on other problems in the town.

And now, I must talk about myself. Detective, I may seem evil and corrupt to you, but you must know that I do not wake up every morning striving to cause havoc in others' lives. I am an excellent con artist and have the skill set to bend others to my will effectively. Am I no different than you in using my gift in the way that I please? However, I must soon bring my letter to a close. Time is of the essence in my current scenario. I do quite enjoy your choice of furniture in your living room though. Very homey. I shall leave you with a few words, Detective. Stay the course of justice, for if you do not, I will have lost the only opponent who ever challenged my ability. Busy yourself with good citizens and their many unfortunate problems. I look forward with excitement *to our next meeting—when the final chapter of our duel will come to a close, and a victor will at last be crowned.*

Your Humble Opponent,
Neil Conway

NEXT FROM GRAYSON SCOTT:

MATTERS OF FACT

A RECOUNTANCE FROM THE PERSONAL EXPERIENCE OF PROFESSOR EVERETT J. ABRAMS

A few persons have endeavored, through various means, to identify the author of what has become known as the "Smith Trilogy". The public has shown increasing interest in this area, and it is due to this fact that I have decided to relinquish my anonymity. Many intriguing cases flood into the hands of the good detective, and most of them will probably be written by his personal chronicler, who is, incidentally, me. For there to be some measure of trust between the public and myself, I have compiled the case which brought both of us together and hope that it will do the deed of silencing those rumors that have been floating around. So now, with pen in hand, I turn to the beginning of the story that shook a countryside, and introduced me to who is, without a fragment of a doubt, the most amazing man that I have ever met.

I. PROFESSOR EVERETT J. ABRAMS

My name, as it appears at the top of this document, is Everett James Abrams. I was previously a resident of the sleepy, quaint, mountainous town of Pagosa Springs, Colorado. For those of my readers who pride themselves on good memory, you will notice that I lived in the same town that was mentioned in "The

Methodology of Detective Smith" as being the starting point for his many adventures. I loathe leaving a loose end hanging this early into my narrative, but we will come back to that point later. I grew up in the British metropolitan of London and my childhood was much like anyone else. I was your typical child with one exception. My father was addicted to the mind, how it worked, what it thought in certain situations, you name it. For the majority of my life I dwelt in the certainty that I would follow in his footsteps. Well, my father happened to be correct. Once I was old enough, I left England altogether and became a student of the prestigious Harvard where I studied psychology and sociology. Four years later, I became one of the youngest teachers to ever teach in that institute. Hence, the "Professor". The job was satisfactory and the salary adequate, but my desire was always to open up my own practice as a psychologist to provide my services to those in need. A few years of teaching gave me enough money to relocate to almost any city of my choosing. I realized that the town of Pagosa Springs did not, in any way, have a professional psychologist on hand. So, with my mind firmly made, I packed up and moved to the Rockies. It did not take long before someone's cousin's sister had heard about my occupation and was willing to rent out a small building to meet my needs. It should be noted that the population of Pagosa Springs is around twelve hundred. Within two weeks, everyone in the city had heard my story and knew my name. My practice had progressed much as any new business does. A few brave souls ventured to employ me and were, much to my pleasure, pleased with my work. Ever since, I have had a steady flow of patients in need of someone to talk to and give their burdens towards. In consultation of my notes, I remember that one of these persons came to visit sometime during the middle of the week.

"Professor, you…you've got to help me!" my client, Robert Huston, cried before there were three inches between the door and the hinge. I do not consider myself an expert on the art of deduction, but even someone as inexperienced as I could be enlightened to the tone of anxiety and utter despair that filled the voice of the person in front of me. Throwing open the door farther, I realized that Mr. Huston had changed since the last time I saw him. In weeks past he had almost always been immaculate in his dress. Suits of the utmost quality adorned his person and he wore an expression of someone who has arrived at the pinnacle of their career. Mr. Huston was a defense attorney of decent caliber that worked most of the criminal cases in town. His track record was rather impressive, if you are into that sort of thing. But because he had to defend some of the worst that mankind has to offer, it brought his state of mind, and conscience, into a state of disarray. Thus, he required my talents to help "set his heart at ease", as he put it. I thought that he was making progress, but as I looked upon his face I had to reconsider. Sweat was practically pouring down his brow, his tie was hanging around his neck untied, and his socks and shoes did not match in the least. This might seem unimportant to someone uninformed, but to me who knew my clients well, this was the first sign that pointed to trouble.

"Mr. Huston, come in, come in. Please. Is everything alright?" I asked with genuine concern. After glancing over his shoulder, my client nearly ran through the front door. I followed Robert Huston to my living room where I motioned him to take a seat. He attempted to sit still, but eventually gave it up and began pacing around the room while running his hand through his hair.

"No, everything is not alright! I…I'm not sure where to start. I'm losing my mind, Professor!" I handed him a glass of water and gently guided him back into his chair.

"Try to calm yourself. Once you feel ready, tell me what has happened." Huston took a few deep breaths before launching shakily into his story.

"You'll have to bear with me for a while here…I'm not that good at telling stories. Ok, well here goes. It all started two weeks ago when I got a message from my assistant telling me that a woman needed a defense attorney. Something about being caught breaking into a random fabric store. I didn't care anything about that though. All I wanted was the payout. Look, my job isn't to know every single detail about the person's crime, ok? The only thing I have to do is break down the prosecutor's attack. I hadn't had a case in months so….so I decided to take it. Everything was normal at first. Got her to sign the contract, got a basic idea of the prosecutor's plan, looked at the evidence, etc. But…but then it started." He jumped up from his seat and grabbed his briefcase that was lying on the floor. I heard a faint click and the top popped open. Inside were bundled groups of small papers held together by various means. One of these he picked up and unraveled. "I started receiving letters…these letters...that scared me outta my wits." I walked over and read one of these aforementioned documents. Here is a representation:

GIVE UP YOUR CLIENT.
IT'S FOR YOUR OWN WELL BEING.

This, shockingly, was one of the more tame notes. I now understood completely my client's condition.

"When did you first receive them?" I asked. This quickly was turning into a police matter, so I postulated that a little detective work would harm no one.

"I got the first one two days after I took my client on. I have…no idea how they got to me. It's not like I go around posting my mailing address to the whole town," Huston cried with almost more despair then previous. He put his head between his hands and looked as if he was on the verge of absolute weeping. Upon seeing this, I endeavored to console my client. However, all of my reassurances fell on deaf ears, was my client so absorbed in his thoughts. It took some fifteen minutes until Huston was able to speak again.

"Why do you not drop the case? Wouldn't the letters stop?" I said with as much passive persuasion I could muster. Huston immediately composed himself and set a gaze on me that riveted all my attention.

"You don't understand, Professor, it's not that easy."

"Mr. Huston, if you are being threatened and have reason to believe the sender will act on his threats, then the only course I can think of is to go to the authorities," I explained.

"I don't know if they'll take me seriously, but I think you're right. I'll go first thing in the morning." Robert Huston proceeded to jump out of his seat and quit the building before I had the opportunity to suggest anything further.

The remainder of the day yielded no more excitement. Once my client had exited, I was left alone with my thoughts. I fell asleep that night with a foreboding feeling deep within me. That feeling soon was justified. The following morning was just like many others. I met with two or three clients and attempted to sift through the always mysterious inner workings of the mind. As I was finishing up my analysis on my latest client, I heard a knock on my door. A quick glance at my timepiece showed that my visitor was not a patient. I pulled on the doorknob and swung the wooden door open. A man and a woman, both in professional dress, stood before me.

"Abrams?" the man grunted."Yes?" I responded, my curiosity aroused.

"Name's Inspector Calhan Reims, this is Rina Welsh," the man named Reims said, nodding toward his companion. Shaking his hand ensured me a few moments to scrutinize my two newest guests. Reims, "the inspector", was a bull doggish, hard featured man of approximately thirty-seven years old with a clean cut way of speech. His partner, Rina Welsh, wore a more friendly expression. Her brown hair was pulled back but I could see that, when full length, most likely reached her elbows. She looked to be roughly thirty-three. I extrapolated that she was the more inexperienced of the two.

"Please disregard my abruptness, but what is the nature of your visit?" I questioned.

"Are you familiar with a man by the name of Robert Huston?" Reims shot back. It did not take much brain power to piece together what might have happened. But I still wondered at what horrible event befell my unfortunate patient.

"I am. He is a patient of mine. He has been coming regularly for the past few months."

"Well, Professor, I am sorry to inform you that Mr. Huston's body was found this morning," Welsh explained. This statement hit me hard. I could not help but feel somewhat responsible. He had come to me in his time of need and yet, the event that he had feared had happened.

"What happened?" I asked. Welsh risked a look at her superior before answering.

"That, sir, is what we are here to find out," she spoke tentatively.

"I will assist in any way that I can," I offered. The bull dog of a man gave a sharp laugh.

"Don't worry, I think that we'll get along well enough without you," he snickered. Welsh rolled her eyes and gave me an apologetic look.

"Oh, give him a chance, will you? We can't be certain of anything yet," she said. Both inspectors ignored my confounded countenance and strode past the threshold and into the house. I trailed them inside and noticed with growing nervousness how they were critically analyzing every aspect of my abode.

"So, how was the murder committed?" I questioned innocently. Reims, without making eye contact, addressed my question.

"Single gunshot wound to the head. Execution style. Looks like whoever killed him wanted to make a point."

"Execution style? I was under the impression that only mobsters and hit men used that signature," I suggested helpfully.

"True, unless someone else wants us to think that. Get us off the track, give him time to get outa town." Reims tone had changed to border line hostility and he had walked slowly closer to me as he spoke until there was hardly two inches between us. Welsh looked as if she was going to intervene, but thought better of it and did not move a muscle.

"Inspector, what exactly are you implying?" I threw at him. His tone had caught me off guard and put me on edge.

"I am implying, *Professor*, that you are currently the number one suspect for the murder of Mr. Robert Huston."